And There Came Forth a Great Fish

STORIES

Tom Weller

Gateway Literary Press

Book design by Robin Basalaev-Binder

Library of Congress Cataloging-in-Publication Data

Names: Weller, Tom, author.
Title: And There Came Forth a Great Fish: Stories / Tom Weller.
Description: First Edition / St. Peters, MO: Gateway Literary Press [2022]
Identifiers: ISBN 9781087976990

First Edition Paperback January 2022
Published by Gateway Literary Press
Gatewayliterarypress.wordpress.com

AND THERE CAME
FORTH A GREAT
FISH

For Kyoko

Contents

Dead Weight

Shortest Marriage.
Bridegroom Robert N____, 39,
collapsed at the altar just as he and
the former Miss Naom N____, 46,
were pronounced man and wife on
September 11, 1976, at the Fort
Palmer United Presbyterian
Church, Greensburg, Pennsylvania.
--Guinness Book of World Records, 1978

Forget everything you've heard about dead weight. It's all lies.

Bobby's a big man. Six feet, three inches, broad shouldered, thick as a Frigidaire, but I scooped him up off the altar floor like I would a fallen baby. I held him against me, rocked him in my arms. Light. Easy. In death Bobby was dandelion fluff, butterfly wings. I felt the last of his heat rippling through my wedding dress. I felt all the hopes and doubts of that day still rattling through my heart.

Do you remember walking through childhood carnivals clinging to a single red helium balloon bought from a man who looked down on his luck? Do you remember wandering the chaotic midway, barkers shouting, music pounding, that balloon pulling you, a feeling buoyant and electric, fragile magic you wanted to hold forever? Do you also remember wanting to let go, wanting to watch that balloon soar?

On that altar, in my arms, Bobby's veins filled with something lighter than air. I held him by the leg of his rented tuxedo pants as he floated up, up, the light of the stained-glass windows dappling his skin in rainbows, the fabric of those pants as slippery as memories against my fingertips.

On that altar, Bobby was that carnival balloon.

That's the truth about dead weight.

Apple Stories

After Mommy disappeared, Shirley's father introduced her to the magic of apple peeling. Fall afternoons, sitting on the back steps, knife in hand, hunched over an apple like a jeweler inspecting a diamond, her father narrated the process as he worked. "You go slow. You go easy. It's not a race. Think about turning the apple. Let the knife do the work. Think thin. Pay attention. Each apple has a story to tell. Think narrow, think fine. That's how you make the peel longer. That's how you make the story special and clear." Finally, he would sit up, lean back, raise his hands, a man presenting an offering to the universe. In his left hand would sit the apple, transformed, naked white flesh glistening in the hazy fall light, apple sweetness perfuming the air. The peel would dangle from his right hand, a single, continuous ribbon, puddling on the ground near Shirley's feet. "Separating the sweet from the bitter. That's the thing about peeling apples," Shirley's father would say.

Eventually, Shirley's father handed her his knife and an unpeeled apple. "Go for it." He stood behind her, silent, as she tried to curl her body into her father's peeling hunch. Still, she heard her father's voice the whole time she worked, his instruction crowding out the voices of her fourth-grade classmates asking questions about Mommy, questions that collected like stormwater in the folds of her brain each school day. *You go slow. You go easy. It's not a race. Think about turning the apple. Let the knife do the work. Think thin. Pay attention. Each apple has a story to tell.* The knife felt awkward in her hand, the handle too thick, the blade reluctant against the flesh of the apple. Her peel kept breaking. A rain of apple peel chips gathered around her feet. Still, her father remained silent until the last of the peel came off: "You know what to do."

Shirley sat up, leaned back, raised her hands. In her left hand sat the apple, white and dimpled with craters and lumps. In her right hand dangled the last three inches of her apple's peel. Shame and disappointment swelled in Shirley's belly. "Ok," her father said. "There it is. Now tonight, you watch the night sky. Watch it real close."

Shirley looked down and studied the shards of apple peel scattered around her feet. Soon they would start to brown, curl like grasping fingers.

*

That night, Shirley lay in bed, fighting off sleep and watching the night sky through her bedroom window. And there it was, a full moon, shiny as chrome and dimpled with craters and lumps, an exact replica of her sorry peeled apple.

*

The next morning, as he worked at the kitchen sink, elbow deep in soap bubbles and breakfast dishes, Shirley's father explained the magic of apples this way: "The past is in the soil and the water. The future is in the dark and the wind. Apples take all of that in, the past and the future, and hold it inside, and when you know how to treat an apple right, it will share this knowledge with you. Just like old ladies whisper home remedies to young mothers, a happy apple will share secrets.

"Apples are simple souls, undemanding. It doesn't take much to make an apple happy. Just a little know-how. Hold the apple gently but caress every inch. Desire the apple. Desire to see its most raw and honest self. Desire to know the apple's secrets. Help the apple reveal itself to you. But don't rush the apple. Go slow. The more patient you are, the more you'll learn, the more details the apple will reveal. Savor the process. The feel of the apple, slick and skittering against your fingertips, the revelation of the apple's shiny white truth, millimeter by silky millimeter, savor it all, every single time. That's all it takes to make an apple happy."

"Can you make the apple tell you important things?" Shirley asked. "Ask it questions like a Magic Eight Ball, only better, not plastic and fake."

"You can try. But it's just like speaking to any wise thing that loves you. You can ask an apple whatever you want. And sometimes an apple will answer your question." Shirley's father paused, held a juice glass slick with rinse water to the sunlight, inspected his work. "And sometimes the apple will only answer the question you should have asked but didn't."

"But then how come my apple showed me the coming of the full moon, but your apples don't ever look like nothing, just round and shiny and perfect?"

"Because I really know how to treat to an apple. Every time I peel an apple with you by my side, I hold in my heart the same question: Apple, will my sweet Shirley love me tomorrow? And when that apple reveals itself, shiny and round and perfect, that apple is telling me that you, Shirley, my one and only sunshine, will be by my side, brightening my life for another day."

*

Shirley practiced making apples happy. Everywhere she went, she carried an apple in her left hand, and all day long, as she bounced through her neighborhood, as she slumped in her school desk watching the minute hand tick across the face of the clock, as she lay in bed fighting off sleep, she spun the apple, her tiny fingers light and electric as a cold breeze dancing across the apple's skin. And Shirley would imagine her fingerprints, sensuous swirls skating across the skin of the apple, marking it, changing it, preparing it to speak.

*

Evenings, Shirley's father would let her take up the knife. First, he would peel, his actions the same, but his words different. Now as he peeled, he would sing to the apple, sing over and over again, "Will my sweet Shirley still love me tomorrow, love me tomorrow?" his voice thick and sweet as corn syrup. The beat changed from day to day. Monday's blues would become Tuesday's rock would become Wednesday's country stomp, and on and on it would go, reggae and gospel and calypso and scat, but the words, the question, remained. And every time the last of the skin would glide free of apple flesh, Shirley's father would lean back, raise his hands, and reveal the truth of that apple, white and shiny and round and perfect.

Then it was Shirley's turn, apple, heavy with fingerprints after a day in Shirley's caress, in the left hand, knife in the right, still awkward, but now familiar. Shirley would wait for her father's directions. "For now, don't worry about asking the apple a question. For now, just concentrate on what you're doing. Let the apple tell the story it wants to tell. Go slow and easy. Apples appreciate if you put in the care to get the peel off in one piece. Let the knife do the work. Go for it."

Shirley would start with the tip of the knife. Close to the stem, steel punctured skin, kissed the flesh, then a twist of the wrist, the slow rotation of the apple, skin freed, flesh revealed. Every passing second, more flesh revealed. And Shirley was patient, willing to devote hours to an apple, willing to forgive herself and push on when the peel broke. And at first the peel always broke, six times on a single apple. Then five times. Four. Three.

And the apples did speak, simple things at first. Reminders of the past: an apple that looked exactly like the rock Shirley had stubbed her toe on just that morning. An apple with exact heft and feel of the snowball Shirley had made last winter and kept stored in the freezer. And a few apples even shared messages from the future. There was the peeled apple that Shirley and her father both agreed looked exactly like an onion. And, sure enough, that night, Mrs. Dawson came by to gift Shirley and her father a five-pound bag of Vidalias. Mrs. Dawson explained that she had bought the onions but couldn't use them because Mr. Dawson refused to eat them, said it wasn't natural or right for an onion to be so sweet. The whole time Mrs. Dawson spoke, Shirley stared at the peeled, onion-shaped apple resting like a totem in the middle of the kitchen table.

After the Vidalia incident, as Shirley's father came to call it, Shirley began to ask her apples questions. Shirley never spoke her inquiries aloud, but before she put knifepoint to apple, she'd concentrate on a single question, hold that question in her heart until she could feel it flapping like a bat caught in a net behind her sternum. As she'd start to peel, she'd feel the question pumping from her center, running down through the veins of her left arm, down into her fingertips, and soaking into the apple spinning against her knife.

At first Shirley only asked questions about the past, questions about the comings and goings of her school friends. This seemed safe, less dangerous than conjuring portents, yet still charged with the electricity of peeking in neighbors' windows. But the apples seemed to have their own agendas and provided Shirley only information she hadn't asked for. Once Shirley asked: *Why did Missy Dawson stop playing with me last year*, but ended up with a peeled apple that looked like a pair of balled socks. That night, Shirley found herself folding her laundry. Each pair of socks felt like a jab in the ribs.

Do what Daddy does. This became Shirley's plan. She decided if she always asked the same question, maybe, the apples would relent, finally answer her in a proper way. Maybe she could pester the truth out of an apple. And she knew just which question to ask, a question so big and heavy that she thought it might bust right through the walls of her heart, split the organ open like an overripe melon.

Shirley took on the bigness of the question, held it inside her, never voicing it. She felt the walls of her heart stretching like a balloon, and she let her heart pump that big question through her veins, through the tips of her fingers, into the flesh of an apple, into the flesh of bushels of apples. Shirley's question? *Where oh where has Mommy gone?*

Where oh where has Mommy gone?

Three ribbons of peel and a naked apple curved like a kidney bean.

The ghost of last night's chili rumbled in Shirley's stomach.

*

Where oh where has Mommy gone?

Two ribbons of peel and a naked apple shaped like a fist.

The sting of a two-year-old punch sizzled Shirley's shoulder, a vision of Missy Dawson's face, red as an apple, after Shirley called Mrs. Dawson fat.

*

Where oh where has Mommy gone?

Two ribbons of peel and a naked apple shaped like a hunching fat bunny.

Poor Mr. Hippity died from an overdose of happiness, Shirley's father had said; eaten by neighborhood dogs, Missy Dawson had hissed.

*

Where oh where has Mommy gone?

A single ribbon of peel, wide as a dime, but perfect, whole, and an apple become a white, glistening, inscrutable rectangle.

A chalkboard eraser from school? An ice cream sandwich? As she tried to read the apple, a buzzing swarm of hornets filled Shirley's head. *A block of government cheese?*

"What do you see, Daddy?"

"A fat letter? A rich lady's wallet?"

They left the naked rectangle apple in the center of the kitchen table, left it where they could see it, ponder it, try to tease out its message as it slowly browned.

*

Where oh where has Mommy gone?

A single ribbon of peel narrow as a shoelace, and long. Shirley imagined wrapping it around her face, an apple peel mummy. A glistening apple rectangle. The same, but different. Its longest surfaces marked with rows of parallel squares, tiny perfect squares. Tiny, perfect, inscrutable squares.

A kind of fancy cleaning sponge? The sole of a clubbed-toe shoe? Part of a waffle iron? The hornets in Shirley's head hummed like electricity.

"What do you see, Daddy?"

"I see a building. A building with tiny windows. Windows just big enough to remind everyone inside what they are missing on the outside."

They set the second rectangle apple on the kitchen table. Like twin sisters, the apples were the same size, but different.

"These apples are trying to say something special to you, Shirley."

*

Where oh where has Mommy gone?

A single ribbon of peel thin as kite string. Shirley imagined it being pulled up, up, up, into the sky, could almost feel it rising through her fingers. A glistening apple rectangle with rows of tiny parallel squares along the longest surfaces, but different. Lines, horizontal and vertical, scarring every surface, a brickwork pattern. Among the bottom rows of squares, a rectangle. A door?

A building? What building? A warehouse? A factory? The hornets in Shirley's head swirled like water racing for the drain.

Shirley carried the naked building apple cradled in both hands. She placed it on the kitchen table with the other rectangle apples.

Shirley's father said, "That apple is the state mental hospital."

All the hornets whooshed from Shirley's head, a panic of wings and gold escaping, leaving only a darkness thick and sticky as tar.

*

"Why is Mommy in the state mental hospital, Daddy?"

"What makes you think Mommy is in there?"

"The apple. Every apple has a story to tell."

"What makes you think this apple's story is about Mommy?"

"I wanted to know what happened to Mommy. I let that question grow in my heart, let that question flow into the apple. I made my apples real happy."

"Sometimes mommies just get tired. Sometimes mommies need help." Shirley's daddy swayed like some heavy thing inside of him had come loose and was swinging wildly back and forth, equilibrium erased, as he talked.

"What's gonna happen to Mommy?"

Shirley reached for the knife before her father even put the apple in her hand.

*

Shirley did the peeling, but they both did the singing. Later Shirley's father would say that Shirley started the singing, and he just followed along. Shirley would say her father started, and she just jumped in. The truth was the song was born in each of their mouths at the exact same moment.

"What's gonna happen to Mommy? Oh, what's gonna happen to Mommy." Rhythm like a jug band, harmony like songbirds, they sang as Shirley peeled.

Shirley peeled slow. Shirley peeled easy. She felt the apple whispering against her fingertips. She felt herself desiring the apple's secrets, a feeling like hunger and fear gone feral. Shirley rode that feeling the way dust rides a hurricane.

Peel thin and fine as spiders' thread spun off Shirley's apple. "What's gonna happen to Mommy? Oh, what's gonna happen to Mommy." Shirley imagined apple peel webs. Shirley imagined tiptoeing fearlessly across apple-peel filaments. "What's gonna happen to Mommy? Oh, what's gonna happen to Mommy." Shirley imagined spinning traps out of apples, spinning bridges out of apples. Shirley imagined spinning home out of apples.

"What's gonna happen to Mommy? Oh, what's gonna happen to Mommy." They sang until their voices rasped like sandpaper on driftwood. They sang until they tasted blood in the back of their throats. They sang until the last of Shirley's peel slipped off the butt of her apple. And then they sang no more. And Shirley sat up, leaned back, and raised her hands, a girl presenting an offering to the universe, a girl hopeful, a girl sticky with apple sweetness, a girl scared, a girl reaching for Mommy, a girl with a left hand holding only light and air where a naked apple should be.

Ponko Returns

Longest Time Spent in a Tree
Bungkas climbed up a palm
tree in the Indonesian village of
Bengkes in 1970 and has been there
ever since, living in a nest that he
made from branches and leaves.
Repeated efforts to persuade him to
come down have failed.
--Guinness Book of World Records, 2001

Bungkas saw it all. The boy, thin limbed and barefoot, his dark hair shining like raven feathers, his bare chest the color of wet sand. Bungkas saw the boy's breathing, counted ribs each time the boy inhaled. One. Two. Three. Four. Bungkas still counts those ribs. One. Two. Three. Four.

The boy picked his way along the rocky shore, each movement deliberate, considered, like a man playing his first game of chess. To win, the boy needed to walk the shoreline without getting his feet wet. In the game he had just invented the ocean water was lava, red and fiery, the touch of a single drop instant death.

Beyond the boy Bungkas saw the ocean, churning blues and grays stretching out to the horizon, racing the sky to oblivion. The rays of the setting sun wove through and around everything, stitched ocean to sky, sky to ocean, boy to sky, ocean to boy, boy to ocean, father to son.

*

Bungkas's palm stands alone, atop a low hill bordering the rocky coast of the island, a stone's throw from the exact spot where Ponko played his lava game.

The palm itself is nothing special. Its knobby brown trunk rises twenty meters into the air, spindly against the backdrop of the sky. The fronds burst out of the top of the trunk, each twice as long as a grown man, a canopy ten meters across that looks like an explosion of feathers and chatters like a tangle of bones every time the wind blows.

Gawkers come to see the nest, not the palm. The nest sits in the center of the palm's canopy as odd and obvious as a bad toupee, a sloppily woven bowl of palm fronds as big around as a tractor tire. Over the years the nest has weathered to a dull gray. From a distance, some visitors mistake the nest for an approaching storm. They say they have to be close, almost able to touch the trunk of the palm, before they can make out Bungkas sitting in the center of the nest, the old man as gray and weathered as the nest, as gnarled as the palm's trunk, steadfast among the leaves and the clouds.

*

The fatigue and the weight of his guilt slowed Bungkas's climb the night he first made his home in his tree. The bark of the trunk chafed his hands and thighs. Sweat stung his eyes and threatened his grip on the palm. With a clattering of leaves Bungkas settled into the canopy. He took a deep breath, felt his ribs straining against his skin. The dark world spread out before him. From the top of the tree Bungkas could see into infinity. Alert, he waited for Ponko.

*

Sudomo was the first to visit the tree. He appeared with the first sunrise. Had Bungkas turned his gaze toward the noise below him, he would have recognized Sudomo immediately. His squat frame, the way he rested his hands on his protruding belly, big as a stewpot, soft as clay, these were as familiar to Bungkas as the air in his own lungs. The two men had known each other since before they had known memory. Born on the same rainy night, they had never lived separated by more than three huts.

"Bungkas, what are you thinking? Aini is sick with worry. Climb down, call Ponko, and we'll return to the village together."

Bungkas called: "*PON KO*," his voice rippling out over the ocean, his voice shaking the bones in Sudomo's chest.

"Where is the boy?" Sudomo yelled.

"*PON KO*," Bungkas called, the sound of his voice eloquent as a siren.

Sudomo lingered by the base of Bungkas's tree. With the toe of his shoe he traced patterns in the dirt. He looked like a man trying to imagine the shape of his best friend's heartbreak.

*

Aini was the second person to visit the tree. Bungkas was certain.

It must have happened near the end of his first week in the tree. Bungkas had already started to lose track of the days.

As Bungkas peered over the ocean's surface and listened to the water, more apathetic than usual, licking the rocks of the coast, he smelled a sweetness in the air. He didn't have to look down to identify the cause of the rustling at the base of his tree. He couldn't bring himself to look down. It was Aini. He could feel her. Ever since she had given birth to Ponko, Bungkas had been able to feel Aini's presence the same way he felt the sun warm against his cheek or the cool ocean air dancing down his spine. At that moment he realized Aini must be able feel him, too.

Bungkas called down, but as he started to speak his tongue swelled. He said "Ai," but that was all he got out before his tongue filled his mouth, swallowed his voice.

Bungkas sat mute, maybe for minutes, maybe for hours, time in the tree so much more slippery than time on the ground. Then, a chattering of leaves, a sound like a bird taking flight. Bungkas saw the rope, a knot the size of a fist on the end, burst through the canopy of the tree, arch lazily over a thick palm frond, and drop back toward the ground.

Bungkas waited until sunset, long after he felt Aini leave, long after his tongue returned to its usual size. He pulled on the rope, pulled until he brought up a dented silver bucket. Bungkas recalled bathing baby Ponko in that very bucket.

In the bucket, he found a bundle of banana leaves. As he cupped the bundle in his hands, he felt Aini's presence, faint but tangible, the way the heat of the sun can be felt in a stone. He unwrapped the bundle, flakey white flesh of steamed fish. His stomach welcomed the fish the way a mother welcomes home a lost child.

From that night on, every night he felt Aini at the base of the tree, every night he lowered the bucket to earth. Every night Bungkas was fed.

*

The gawkers always come early in the morning, before the heat of the day, or at dusk, when cool breezes blow in from the ocean as the light begins to fade.

Bungkas's friends gawked first. They came during his first year in his tree. They all called up to him.

Some called in cooing, rhythmic voices, "Bung kas, oh Bung kas, come down. Bungkas come hooomme." They called to Bungkas in the voices of coaxing old women.

Others spoke like old men snapping at stubborn children. "Get. Down. Now. Aini. Needs. You." Each word cracking the air like a pistol shot.

Still others called in the same easy voices they had always used to share stories with Bungkas around morning fires. "Bungkas, you have got to come down and get a look at Sudomo. I swear, his belly grows larger every day. Any minute now, he will give birth. It's probably twins." Then laughter like a cock's crow.

Sometimes Bungkas wanted to call down to his friends, to ask them not to worry or to just share in their laughter. But he never could. Always his tongue would swell, strange magic, rendering him mute.

*

Right before the stranger gawkers started to appear, Bungkas saw Ponko. Not the boy, exactly, but still Ponko.

Bungkas hurt. His knees and shoulders and hips all ached. He could find no comfortable position for sitting. The muscles of his neck felt tight as coiled springs as he strained to distinguish ocean from dark sky.

He listened to his stomach growling, felt it twist in on itself. Quick as a hiccup, the thought appeared: *Maybe it's time. Maybe it's over.*

But then Ponko, but not exactly Ponko. Something far in the distance, hovering along the line where ocean met sky. Something like a plume of smoke, but brighter. Something like a plume of smoke made of silver light. It wobbled and shifted, movements whose subtlety spoke of their importance, like the twitching muscles, the measured breathing of a man on a wire.

Then the voice, bright as sleigh bells, not carried on the air, yet still ringing in Bungkas's ears. Ponko's voice: "Wait for me. I will return."

And then it was gone, that thing that was Ponko, but not exactly Ponko, gone as quick as a heart breaks.

*

By the start of his third year, or maybe his fourth, in the tree, Bungkas didn't recognize any of the gawkers. He still heard them, though they mostly spoke to each other now.

"How long?"

"Why?"

"Say he lost his boy."

Their words sparked and snapped, a live wire running through the gawkers.

"Looks like a pile of rags"

"Why?"

"Crazy."

"Crazy as a bedbug."

"Crazy as a shithouse rat."

Then laughter like a hyena pack.

Rarely, they would still call up to Bungkas.

"Hey, Buddy, wadda ya lookin' at?"

"What's the weather like up there?"

"Seen any good clouds lately?"

Bungkas never wanted to call back.

*

As time changed the village, the village changed Ponko's story.

He just wandered off while Bungkas napped, got turned around somehow, lost his way. He's still wandering, somewhere, following the coast, looking for something familiar, a landmark to lead him home.

He ran away, searching for something better. He'd heard the sweet old stories about life on the other side of the island, tales of fair weather and full bellies, fish jumping right out of the ocean and into cook pots. Boys believe such things. Boys get lost in silly dreams.

He ran away. Away from the sting of a switch across the back of his legs, the dull pain in the wake of the slap of Bungkas's rough palm across his ear. He ran away from shameful family secrets, horrors unsuspected by even his closest neighbors.

He just stopped breathing. Nobody knows why. A seizure of some kind, probably. These things happen. Bungkas buried him immediately, there along the shore, Ponko's favorite part of the island. Bungkas sits in his tree, waiting for his heart to heal, keeping vigil over his only child's grave.

It was an accident. They were just wrestling, the way all fathers and sons will, an ancient, innate ritual, boyhood reaching for manhood, when Bungkas felt Ponko go limp in his arms. The way light departs an extinguished candle, just that quick, life left the boy's body, and the pull of gravity increased fourfold. Ponko's little body in Bungkas's arm weighed three hundred pounds. Bungkas buried Ponko there, close to the shore, and then climbed the tree, desperate to rise above his shame.

One blow, that's all it took. The back of Ponko's skull shattering like a ripe melon under the pressure of the stone Bungkas swung in his right hand. A calculated choice born of dangerous arithmetic. One less mouth to feed. One less soul for Aini to nurture. Bungkas would bask in the full light of her attention. With the boy gone life would be better at home. Then a miscalculation realized. With Ponko dead, Bungkas could never go home.

Ponko just wandered off.

*

Many years later, exactly how many impossible to say, time so slippery at the top of a tree, the gawkers began to call to Bungkas again, their voices sweet singsongs, like kind schoolteachers.

"Why did you climb up?"

"Why don't you climb down?"

"What do you see?"

"What do you hope to see?"

Bungkas heard them talking to each other as well, their mingled voices still light and fluttery, a cloud of butterflies.

"Did he say something?"

"Shh. Listen?"

"I think he said something."

"Shh."

"He didn't say anything."

"The circumference of the trunk is exactly thirty-six inches."

"Should I write that down?"

"Write it all down."

"Is that important?"

"It's all important"

"It all must be preserved."

Then, never laughter, just a shared deep intake of breath followed by a silence as stark as an empty church.

*

Stories about Bungkas and his life in the tree bloomed in the mouths of the children and spread throughout the village.

He drinks only rainwater that he wrings out of his long, grey hair.

With his bare hands, he snatches birds out of the sky to eat.

His beard has grown so long that it covers his feet. At night, for warmth, he curls his body against the beard, holds it like a lover.

His fingernails, his toenails have grown long and sharp as tiger claws.

He has been alone in the tree so long that he has forgotten language. That's why he remains silent, no matter who calls up to him.

His years of searching have given Bungkas super vision. He sees into the future. That is why he never comes down. He cannot bear to share what he has seen.

With each passing year the stories of Bungkas became more enmeshed with the life of the village. Parents listening to their children describe Bungkas experienced déjà vu, the pull of nostalgia, tales of the warmth of Bungkas's beard, the burden of his super vision like notes of a favorite childhood song.

*

Before Ponko disappeared, Bungkas saw the wave, foamy, swollen, tumbling in on itself, so much bigger than the boy. But he saw it too late. By the time Bungkas saw the wave it, it had taken Ponko from his lava game, plucked him from the rocky shore, gripped the boy like a fist. The glint of his raven-black hair flashed through the silver foam, wave and boy now one, rushing away from the shore, tumbling toward the setting sun.

Bungkas yelled his son's name: *Ponko*, voice big as a thunderclap. He ran to the shore, did not feel the rocks under his feet, dove into the water, did not feel its chill. He swam and swam, fought the waves and yelled the boy's name until his lungs and arms burned. He swam while darkness engulfed the ocean and played cruel tricks. Swimming through the blackness, Bungkas felt reality twisting all around him. North, south, east, west, distinctions all disappeared, up and down, suddenly matters of conjecture. Bungkas guessed, picked a direction, swam. Ten thousand furious strokes. Five thousand booming cries: *Pon Ko*. Each syllable a prayer.

He fought through the churning water not because he thought he could find the tiny, frail boy in the vastness of the ocean, but because that's all he could do. And that is what fathers do when their sons disappear. They do all they can do.

*

Now, only children come to Bungkas's tree. Adults pass by. Some turn their head skyward, briefly, to find Bungkas, still vigilant among the clouds, like pausing to find the North Star, comfort in consistency. But only children stop to gawk.

They cup their hands around their mouths and shout toward the sky, "Bungkas, Bungkas, Bungkas."

The one-upmanship begins, the game of I-Can-Make-Him-Look.

"BUNGKAS."

"BUNGKAS."

"BUNGKAS, BUNGKAS."

"DIRTY OLD BUNGKAS."

"CRAAY ZEE BUNGKAS."

They run in place, legs and arms churning as they call, desperate to burn off a throbbing energy they only feel when gathered, together, under this tree.

"BUUUUNGKAASSS, I LUUUVV YOU."

Then laughter, together, a chorus of sleigh bells.

And Bungkas's heart swells. From the cocktail of laughter, Ponko rises to embrace Bungkas.

Bungkas dare not move, dare not call down to the children below.

Bungkas sits stock still, laughter swirling around him, and feels Ponko, each silver-bright cackle, a tiny reaching finger against Bungkas's skin.

Bungkas closes his eyes. Bungkas slows his breathing.

Ponko returns.

Bungkas does all he can do.

Squeal

Hiccoughing

The longest recorded attack of hiccoughs was that afflicting Charles Osborne (b. 1894) of Anthon, Iowa, from 1922 to date. He contracted it when slaughtering a hog. His first wife left him and he is unable to keep in his false teeth.

--Guinness Book of World Records, 1978

The blood will be as warm as your morning coffee. But first there is the squeal. It starts before blade touches flesh.

The pig hangs from the killing tree upside down, wiggles and thrashes and squeals, fighting against the hemp rope looped around his rear hooves and cursing the future. The pig's head hangs at your eye level, comes closer and then retreats with each desperate twitch, comes closer and then retreats as if considering a kiss. But it's the squeal that's got you. The squeal is part sawmill buzz and part diesel engine rumble. It is your mother's wailing the first time you broke her heart and the throaty commands of your red-faced father. The squeal grabs your spinal cord with two hands and shakes.

Above the two of you, the late-fall canopy of the killing tree is a riot of reds and oranges, a thing on fire.

You take up your knife, the knife that's as long as your forearm, the knife that feels like a sword, heavy and hungry for blood. You put your knife to the pig's throat.

You speak to the pig, speak words enveloped by the squeal, words simple and heartfelt: *Thank you.* This you owe the pig. This is respect.

You drive knife blade through skin, through fat, through twitching muscles, through pulsing veins, through trachea. You witness blood and breath and squeal abandon pig, life rushing out the way air exits a balloon.

You place an old coffee can under the pig to catch the rushing blood. Waste not. This, too, is respect. You feel the absence of the squeal. You feel the whole world around you changed.

You feel a pressure in your throat, a feeling like a tiny swirling storm has entered you, a feeling like that storm is growing, skies darkening, thunderheads building. You open your mouth to relieve that pressure. You hear the pig's death squeal erupt from your throat. You feel the world shrinking around you. You feel your spine shake.

This first squeal is all power, part trumpet's call, part right cross, part hurricane wind, part wrecking-ball swing, part shotgun blast. This first squeal steals from you, brazen, steals the air from your lungs, the moisture from your tongue, takes the teeth from your mouth and flings them into the graying light of the gathering dusk. You watch your teeth leaving you, a Cheshire cat smile exploded and tumbling through space.

One throat, two voices. One voice angry, scared, human, a rush of *shit*s and *fuck*s and *cocksucker*s, a thrumming flock of *God damn*s. This is the voice you long to hear, pray to hear even while you *God damn.*

One voice angry, scared, dying, porcine, a squeal that shakes your spine even as it escapes your throat. This is the voice you hear.

You feel the squeal roaring up your throat, feel it lunging toward the light, feel it clawing, desperate to be out in the world. But as it crosses your bloody gums, your lips, the boundary lines that mark where you stop and the world begins, you swallow.

Swallowing the dying pig's squeal feels like how you imagine drowning must feel. A weight in your chest, a tightening, you feel as if suddenly your rib cage is one size too small. You feel tingling in the tips of your fingers, tips of your toes. The top of your head crackles and sparks like an electrical fire.

Hiccup. It bursts out of you, sudden like a dragonfly, involuntary like a blink, welcome as a kiss.

Hiccup. Hiccup. Hiccup. Hiccup, persistent as the laughter of children, quicker than a pig's squeal. You now know what the future will bring, can see it spreading out before you like an ocean reaching for the horizon.

You won't stop hiccupping.

You will reach under the dangling pig carcass, pick up the old coffee can half-filled with blood. You will pet the pig carcass on the head, scratch it under the chin. You will think the carcass looks so much like a boxer's heavy bag. You will leave the pig carcass behind.

You won't stop hiccupping.

You will walk back to the house, back to your lover. You will find your lover, back turned toward you, in the kitchen. Your lover will be busy, washing dishes or peeling potatoes. Your lover's hands will be fluttering through the air like two nervous sparrows. You will hiccup and those hands will still. Your lover will turn toward you, see your mouth, toothless, bloodstained. Your lover's eyes will grow big as fists, and your lover will ask, "What happened?"

Hiccup. You will set the coffee can half-filled with this pig's blood on the kitchen counter, a sound like the fall of a gavel. *Hiccup.*

"Try a deep breath. Tell me what happened."

You will dip your right index finger in the pig's blood. You will start to write on the kitchen counter, blood streak letters, red darkening to brown, your printing as precise as surgery. In pig's blood all over your home, you will write for your lover. You will write your story. You will write this story. You will write of death and respect and karma and revenge and choking on the voices of spirits. You will write of the feel of a pig's squeal. And you won't stop hiccupping, and you will keep writing, as long as your lover will have you.

Mouse Drawer

Leon and Fay didn't dance for long that first afternoon in the new house.

Leon dropped the last box from the truck, swooped Fay up in his arms, pulled her close. Together they twirled around the kitchen while Leon hummed "The Tennessee Waltz," accompanied by the creaking of floorboards and the hiss and rattle of pipes buried in the walls. To Fay, Leon smelled like yeast. To Leon, Fay smelled like moist earth. Their sweaty flesh stuck together wherever it met. But neither cared, because they were together, in a place all their own, at last.

"We should open the wine," Fay said.

"Absolutely." Leon leaned down and gave Fay a kiss, her lips plump and slick against his.

"I already put the kitchen stuff away. Dance me over to the cabinets to grab corkscrew."

"Absolutely."

Their feet shuffling across the linoleum floor sounded like pages turning.

Fay kept one arm wrapped around Leon. With the other she groped the air behind her, searching for the handle of the top drawer next to the sink. Leon abandoned "The Tennessee Waltz" and composed a tune of his own. "Bum didi dum did um," he sang, squirming and twisting his head to avoid filling his mouth with Fay's auburn hair.

Fay found the drawer handle, the metal warmed by the sun streaming through the curtainless kitchen window. She pulled.

Leon saw it first. A tiny gray ball of energy shooting out of the open drawer and landing on the floor. Fay saw it next, zipping past Leon, heading toward the backdoor, its movements quick and erratic. Like mercury, it seemed both liquid and solid at the same time.

"What is it?" Fay hissed, clinging tighter to Leon.

"Mouse," Leon said.

Its feet skittering against the linoleum floor sounded like a distant drumroll.

And then it was gone, the noise, the mouse. And Leon held Fay in his arms and said, "It's all right. It's all right."

"Where'd it go?"

"I don't know. You scared it pretty good. I bet it's a long way from here already."

And Fay squeezed Leon, and Leon breathed in the lilac scent of her hair and listened to something that sounded like a faint, distant voice panting, "Our house, our house, our house."

*

Too tired to assemble a proper bed, but too excited to sleep, Fay and Leon spent the first evening in the new house tumbled together in a pile of blankets on the floor, camped in what would become their living room. They watched the world captured in their front windows turn from gray to black, whispered to each other, conjuring the future.

"We should paint the kitchen green," Fay said.

"I bet my mom will give us her old recliner," Leon said.

"We should rip up this tacky carpet."

"I've seen some decent area rugs at the thrift shop on Walnut."

"Maybe add a skylight. In the kitchen. For warmth."

"Skylights are expensive."

And on and on they talked like this, until they could see the place transformed, until they could hear their stomachs rumble.

"Hungry?" Leon said.

"I think we only have cereal," Fay said

*

In the kitchen, Fay poured Cheerios and milk into two bowls. She opened the top drawer next to the sink, reached for two spoons. She slammed the drawer shut. She wasn't quick enough. Fay shrieked and hopped around the kitchen as if her feet were on fire.

Leon burst into the kitchen. "What? What?"

"Another mouse, from the same drawer."

Leon saw it, just like the first, a gray blur, speeding across the floor. "What is with this drawer?" Leon said. He opened the top drawer next to the sink. Two more mice jumped out before he could close it.

The three mice scrabbled across the kitchen floor, hither and yon, like moths caught in a swirling wind. The twelve mouse feet against the linoleum floor sounded like a man clawing against a closed casket lid.

Leon tried to chase after the whirl of mice. He took heavy steps. Two stomps to the right, then three to the left, then two stomps forward. But the mice were everywhere at once. They zipped across the kitchen floor as quick and unpredictable as August lightning.

And then one mouse said, "Why are you in our house?"

And Fay screamed as if she had found a finger floating in her bowl of Cheerios, and Leon yelled, "Your house?"

"Yes," squeaked a second mouse voice. "We were here first."

"Get out!" Leon yelled. He snatched up a broom leaning against the wall.

"Get out!" Fay shrieked as she hopped to the back door, opened it. "Leon, help me!"

Leon swatted at the floor with the broom, over and over again, every blow just missing a mouse.

"But if you chase us out, we'll never leave," came a winded mouse voice.

"Get out!" Fay and Leon both yelled. Their voices rattled the dishes in the kitchen cabinets.

Out the open backdoor all three mice raced, nose to tail, one after the other, a tiny, furry, speeding train, down the back steps, through the flower bed overtaken by weeds, across the tinder-dry lawn, and beyond, off to parts unknown.

Carried on the wind, a chorus of tiny mice voices sung faintly to Leon and Fay: "If you chase us out, we'll never leave."

*

Their first night in the new house, Leon and Fay slept in their jumble of blankets on the floor, curled together like a pair of old housecats. And while their cereal bowls sat in the sink growing sticky with drying milk and silver moonlight streamed in the front windows, washed over their sleeping bodies, Fay and Leon dreamed.

Fay's dream went like this:

Fay is walking through the house. The time of day is unclear, but sunlight fills the front windows. As Fay walks, her footsteps do not creak the floorboards; she does not hear the usual hiss and rattle of the pipes buried in the walls. Instead, all is silence.

As Fay reaches the middle of the living room, she looks down at her feet, and she sees them, three gray mice, lined up nose to tail, circling her feet, their speed increasing with each lap, a tiny, frantic, furry, train.

She looks away quickly, looks up toward a recliner, sees that it is gray. And it is dotted with thousands of tiny black eyes, fringed with thousands of fleshy tails, pulses with thousands of tiny, rapid heartbeats.

Fay turns away from the recliner, looks toward a bookshelf in the corner, only to find even more tiny eyes and tails and throbbing heartbeats. The bookshelf, too, is made of mice.

She looks back toward the carpet, now gray and twitching, thousands of mice, maybe millions, locked together in shifting patterns under her feet. She feels twitching whiskers against her heels, feels breath against her ankles.

Fay opens her mouth to scream, but nothing comes out. She keeps trying to scream, but all is silence, even as she feels a single mouse climbing up her leg, past her chest, onto her shoulder. Even as she feels the mouse's claws poking the flesh of her lips, feels its whiskers against the roof of her mouth, against the back of her throat, all is silence.

Leon's dream went like this:

Leon is on the living room floor, curled in the fetal position, warm and comfortable amidst a jumble of blankets. The silver light of a quarter moon shines in the front windows. The air in the living room is still and carries the smell of Cheerios, earthy and familiar. Leon throws one arm over the blanket-covered body next to him, Fay, curls into her. He listens to Fay's breathing, slow and deep. He feels Fay's heart beating.

Leon slows his breathing so it matches Fay's. Leon pinches his eyes shut, concentrates on his heart. He feels it in his chest, pictures it in his mind, a throbbing knot of muscle the size of his fist. He tries to slow its beating. Leon tries to make his heart beat in time with Fay's.

Leon speaks into the blankets pulled over Fay's head. He tells Fay he is blessed to have her. He tells Fay he will always treasure and protect her. He feels his own breath, moist and hot against the blanket. He tells Fay all he wants in this world is to be with her and to make her happy, and he feels her heart start to beat faster, hears her breathing, short, quick bursts. He feels Fay rolling toward him. He grabs the top of the blanket, pulls it away with a wrist-swirling flourish worthy of a magician. Ta-da.

And Leon unveils a giant gray mouse. Its shiny black eyes are as big as softballs, its front teeth the size of soap cakes, its whiskers like bailing wire, its body a furry torpedo. Leon can't bring himself to look at its tail.

Leon wants to run away, but his legs and arms have gone numb. He feels his heart racing, keeping time with the rapid beat of the giant mouse heart. And then the mouse turns so it's looking Leon dead in the eye, and it opens its mouth, and it speaks, with Fay's voice.

The giant mouse says, "Treasure me, Leon. Make me happy, Leon." And Leon feels something stroking his ankles, and without looking he is sure he is being caressed by a giant mouse tail, thick around as his forearm.

And while they slept, Fay and Leon both struggled and squirmed under the weight of their mouse dreams. Fay reached, grasped, trying to cling to, to climb Leon, for protection, to get away from the mice. Leon wiggled away from Fay, swatted away her grasping hands, to get away from the mice.

And so it would be for Leon and Fay, every night thereafter, the mice they chased away never leaving.

Hercules Massis

Pulling with Teeth.

The "strongest teeth in the world" belong to "Hercules" J____ Massis (b. W____ O____ M____, June 4, 1940 of St. Amandsberg, Belgium), who in October, 1976, demonstrated the ability to pull a locomotive and a truck weighing 135.5 tons on a level track at Park Royal, London, with a bit in his teeth.

--Guinness Book of World Records, 1978

The men have come to hear the snap of a jawbone, to see teeth shatter, gums explode, blood blooming in the air like fireworks. They clap their oil-stained hands, stomp their boots in the gravel lining the tracks. They buy bags of popcorn from a strolling vendor. They yell, "Give 'em hell." They yell, "You can do it, Mate." They pretend they have come to root for Hercules Massis.

They have come to root for the train.

Hercules Massis waves to the men. He flexes his arms, pounds his chest, a sound like a bass drum. He waves again and smiles, shows off his mighty choppers. He pretends the men have come to root for him. He pretends he doesn't feel like a man on a wire.

Hercules takes the bit in his mouth. The metal feels warm against his lips, tastes electric on his tongue. He takes a deep breath, stares down his challenge. An eight-foot length of rope, thick around as a baseball bat, connects the bit in his mouth to the train, one locomotive and two boxcars.

The men grow impatient, their shouts more insistent. "Come on. Let's go." Some complain about the heat of the day. Pigeons scramble among their feet, scavenge dropped popcorn. Hercules closes his eyes, hears only his own voice in his head chanting: "Her. Cue. Lees. Her. Cue. Lees." His heartbeat slows.

A man wearing a bowler hat fires a starter pistol. Pigeons burst into the air. Hercules Massis takes one easy step backward. The rope goes taut.

Through squinted eyes Hercules sees the nose of the locomotive. Blood pounds in his ears. Veins and tendons bulge, furrow the skin of his neck and shoulders. He feels all the weight of the train in his mouth.

The nose of the locomotive is shiny and silver, rounded and sleek. Hercules wants to touch it, to feel its curves warm against his palm. He reaches back with one foot, braces the sole of his boot against the railroad tie. Strains. Nothing. Not even a millimeter. He hears his own voice in his head: "Her. Cue. Lees. Her. Cue. Lees."

The men grow loud. They yell, "Come on, come on." They yell, "You can do it."

Hercules hears a hundred voices yelling, "Break his mouth. Break him." His chest becomes hollow. Lead fills his stomach. Still he strains, against the weight of the train, against the hopes of the men. Hercules wants to lie down and cry.

He feels it first in his ankle. The completion of a tiny backward step. Movement. He hears it first in the change in the men's voices. The tone rises, the words jumble: "Did you see. Oh my God. Can't be. No." Hercules strains again. Boot heel pushes against railroad tie. A subtle rotation of steel wheels, and Hercules hears the train calling to him. Its voice, high-pitched and pretty as birdsong, drowns out the noise of the men. The train says, "I'm coming to you, Hercules. I'm coming." And

Hercules reaches back with his foot again. Another backward step, bigger, easier than before. Momentum. And at that moment, the lead in Hercules's stomach becomes three hundred butterflies, and his hollow chest fills with helium. For the first time in his life Hercules Massis is in love. He wants to run to the train and stroke it, whisper promises and thanks to it. But he knows he must wait. There will be time for that later, away from the crowd. For now, they must dance, Hercules leading, the train following, moving together to a chorus of disappointed men's voices mumbling conjecture about fakery.

Tomorrow morning the newspapers will proclaim, **Hercules Massis, Man with the World's Strongest Teeth.** They will trumpet the numbers: 135 tons pulled over ten meters. But Hercules Massis will remember only the sound that train made as it rolled down the track, "Her. Cue. Lees. Her. Cue. Lees," calling to him, insistent, uninhibited, the way lovers do, and the way a bit in the mouth can feel just like a kiss.

Faith and Flight

Flight

Father Al will not fly like Superman. He will not zip through the sky on his belly, hands extended as if stretching for something forever just out of reach. Father Al will not spin and bank like a fighter jet. Father Al will not be faster than a speeding bullet.

When Father Al flies, it will be more like his blood has been replaced with helium, and he has no choice but to leave the ground and no control over what happens after that.

The Miracle Man

Father Al is the scariest priest Graham has ever met.

Father Al is old. Graham doesn't know how old exactly but he does know Father Al's head is completely bald and dotted with brown spots, and he has really pale skin, skin the color of milk, and it hangs in strange folds and flaps around his neck, almost like his skin is trying to slither off his face, Graham thinks. Father Al is tall, the tallest priest Graham has ever met, with long, thin arms and legs. He mostly reminds Graham of a withered daddy longlegs.

And Graham hates being an altar boy for Father Al.

Masses follow a script. There's always the readings and then the homily and then the communion, in that order. And the script is important for the altar boys because that is how they know the right time to hold the big red book so the priest can read from it or to bring the water for the priest to wash his hands before touching the Eucharist or to ring the bells. Knowing the script and following the script is what keeps Graham from making a mistake while up on the altar in front of St. Paul's whole congregation.

But knowing the script isn't much help for Graham when Father Al is saying mass. Father Al often forgets things. Sometimes he forgets little things. Sometimes when it's time to sing, he forgets to turn off the mic that he wears pinned to his robe, so instead of hearing the whole church singing all Graham can hear is Father Al's deep, gravelly voice, and it sounds to Graham more like Father Al is yelling at kids to keep off the church lawn, rather than singing to praise God. Other times Father Al forgets big stuff, whole parts of the script, important parts, like the homily or the prayers of the faithful. Then it becomes really difficult for Graham to know what to do, and if he ends up not bringing the big red book or the water to wash when Father Al wants it, Father Al glares at Graham as if Graham is amazingly stupid, right up there by the altar, in front of the whole congregation, with the big plaster Jesus hanging on the cross behind Graham looking down on him, Jesus with his eyes closed, his head drooping, as if Graham's mistakes are wearing him out.

So you can understand why Graham will be surprised when Father Al is the vessel for the miracle. You can understand why Graham will be so surprised when Father Al flies.

Flight Preparations

It is just a regular Sunday mass. Graham sits in one of the little chairs off to the side of the altar, where the altar boys always sit. Jack Kubiak, the other altar boy this Sunday, sits next to Graham. Jack smells like a bonfire of cheap cologne, like Old Spice or Aqua Velva licked by flames, because Jack has started smoking and he thinks the cologne hides the scent of the cigarettes.

Graham's mom stands in front of the altar, way over to the left side of the church, behind a microphone, facing the congregation to lead the singing, just like she does most Sundays. Graham's dad stands in the back with the other ushers, just like he usually does. Graham's family has the whole church covered. They are famous at St. Paul's. They've been coming to St. Paul's since Graham was a baby. It always takes Graham's family at least twenty minutes to get to their car after mass because everybody has to stop them to say hi and complain about the weather and comment on how fast Graham is growing.

Father Al walks to the lectern. He reads the Gospel. He starts his homily. Today, he seems to remember the script.

As Father Al gives his homily, he speaks so loudly into the mic that what he says is a rumble, sounds like traffic instead of words.

Graham's Secret

Graham is not listening to Father Al's homily. He is not thinking about Father Al or church or God during mass. He usually doesn't. He tries to, but it almost never works. Instead, he mostly thinks about superheroes. He makes up stories in his head, stories that he would like to see in comics but knows he never will. He tries to imagine what would happen if Wolverine fought Superman. He tries to imagine what would happen if Captain America turned evil and decided to kill the president.

Takeoff

As Father Al gives his homily, Graham imagines what might have happened if Peter Parker had been stung by a radioactive bee instead of being bitten by a radioactive spider. Graham tries to imagine Beeman, the way he might look, the powers he might have, and then he hears, boom, boom, boom, Father Al's heavy footsteps as he walks away from the lectern. Graham looks at Father Al, tries to forget Beeman, because, as long as Father Al remembers the script, he will start getting communion ready soon, and there will be work for the altar boys to do.

But then Graham hears nothing, no footsteps, but Father Al still moves across the altar. So Graham watches Father Al's steps, and they are the same big steps he always takes, his long legs unwinding like whips. But his feet don't touch the floor.

Father Al flies. For two more steps his feet never touch the shiny marble of the chancel floor. They hover centimeters above it. And then Father Al is back on the ground, and Graham feels in his chest the boom, boom, boom of Father Al's steps as he continues to walk. And Graham feels a tingling in his stomach because he has just witnessed a miracle. And Graham's mother flips through her hymnal, preparing to sing. And Graham's father twirls the long-handled collection basket he holds in his hands, like a pools shark fiddling with his cue. And Graham looks up at the plaster Jesus hanging on the cross behind the altar, and the plaster Jesus looks down at Graham.

Graham's Bigger Secret

Graham started thinking about superheroes at mass because he hopes that is better than thinking about women, which used to happen a lot and still sometimes happens. Mostly, he thinks about Mrs. Harrold, the most beautiful mom at St. Paul's. She has red hair and shiny white teeth, the thin, tight frame of a former pageant girl, breasts that remind Graham of grapefruits. Sometimes when Mrs. Harrold sees Graham's family leaving mass, she'll stop them to say hi and tell Graham how fast he is growing. Sometimes she will put her hand on Graham's shoulder, and it always feels warm and electric.

Graham knows that he shouldn't be thinking about women during mass, but it is hard not to. Graham figures that maybe God is testing him, putting the thoughts in his head to tempt him, to see if they distract him or if Graham will focus on mass and praying.

Graham used to worry that he failed the test, spectacularly, but now knows that God is truly loving, so loving that God must grade on curve, because Graham must have passed the test, because God showed him Father Al flying. God showed him a miracle.

Touchdown

Graham wants to shout as soon as Father Al settles back to Earth, wants to yell Hallelujah or Praise God or Holy cow, did you see that? But Graham does not yell because you can't do that at mass. Graham has never seen anyone yell inside of St. Paul's, unless Father Al's singing with the mic on counts as yelling.

Dear God

Graham goes straight to his room when he gets home from mass. He kneels by his bed, props his elbows on his mattress, joins his hands, and prays, just as he used to, many years ago, before he started thinking about women at mass:

Dear God, it's me, Graham, and yes, I know that you already know that, but it's really hard to find a good way to start a prayer, but, of course, you already know that too, and you know, of course, that I saw Father Al fly, because you made sure I saw it, because you wanted me to see it.

I'm so grateful that you showed me a miracle. I think that will change me forever, make me a better person. I'm sure when I'm at mass now I will not be thinking about superheroes or anything else that I'm not supposed to be thinking about. I will only be thinking about the mass and about you, God, because you have shown me something incredible. You have called me personally. At least that's what I think happened, but I also worry that it could be Satan making me see things or maybe this is another test from you that I'm not understanding right now. I've got a lot to think about, but I know you'll help me figure this out and that you'll help those who help themselves.

Anyway, thanks for a great mass. It was awesome.

Amen.

Seeker

Graham uses the computer in the family room. He researches, just like he did for his science project about manatees, when starchy old Ms. Owens kept telling him, Graham, I want you to learn how to find your own answers, every time he tried to ask her something about manatees.

Google Search: "flying priests"

BBC NEWS | World | Americas | **'Flying' priest's** balloons found

Apr 23, 2008 ... Search crews off Brazil's coast find the balloons that were being used by a missing **priest** trying to set a flight record.

news.bbc.co.uk/1/hi/world/americas/7360416.stm - 51k - Cached - Similar pages

National Association of **Priest** Pilots

Since its humble beginnings in the 1964, the National Association of **Priest** Pilots has become an international group of "**Flying Priests**.

...

*www.**priest**pilots.org/ - 21k* - Cached - Similar pages

Brazil **priest flying** party balloons lost at sea | U.S. | Reuters

Apr 22, 2008 ... BRASILIA (Reuters) - A Brazilian **priest** is missing after he drifted out to sea while trying to set a record for a flight using helium-filled ...

www.reuters.com/article/newsOne/idUSN2228192120080422 - 63k - Cached - Similar pages

wcr:01/29/01 -- **Flying** Fathers: Hockey-playing **priests** out to ...

Jan 29, 2001 ... Coming soon to Alberta are the **Flying** Fathers, an internationally famous team of hockey-playing **priests** who over the past 39 years have ...

*www.wcr.ab.ca/news/2001/0129/**flying**012901.shtml - 12k* - Cached - Similar pages

Leftover **Flying**: **Priests** to purify site after Bush visit

The sky/ never fills with any/ leftover **flying**." -Li-Young Lee, from Praise Them ... **Priests** to purify site after Bush visit. Read all about it. ...

*paulacisewski.blogspot.com/2007/03/**priests**-to-purify-site-after-bush-visit.html - 29k* - Cached - Similar pages

Graham thinks, *nothing good.* Graham thinks, *it's all junk.*

Dear Mom

Mom stands by the kitchen sink. Her hands move furiously. She is a carrot peeling machine. The peeler makes a clicking noise that Graham likes.

Have you ever seen a miracle? Graham asks her.

Mom's hands don't slow down, not even for a second. The peeler keeps clicking, clicking, clicking, doesn't miss a beat.

I think I've seen lots of miracles, she says. I think they're around us every day. The colors in the sunrise, the laughter of children, all those kinds of things, and lots of other things, too. Those are all kind of miracles, don't you think?

I saw Father Al fly, Graham says.

The clicking of the peeler stops. Mom looks at Graham as if waiting for him to deliver a punch line. Graham feels his face growing hot.

Come on, she says.

For real, Graham says.

You may be spending too much time with your comic books, Mom says.

Dear Dad

Graham's family won't eat until they pray. Dad leads: Bless us, oh Lord, and these thy gifts. . .

It's the same prayer Graham has said before every meal since he first learned to speak. It used to be that saying the prayer before eating didn't even feel like talking for Graham. It was more like just making sounds, something he did not even have to think about, a learned instinct like yelling a warning when you see something bad is about to happen.

But tonight, the prayer feels different to Graham. It is as if he I can feel the words, vibrating, pulsing, alive, in his mouth as he speaks them.

As soon as the prayer is finished, Dad reaches for the pork chops, and Mom reaches for the mashed potatoes, and Graham does what he feels called to do.

What do you think about miracles? Graham says to Dad.

Oh, Graham, not this again, Mom says.

Not what again, Dad says.

I saw a miracle.

Really, Dad says. What kind of miracle?

I saw Father Al fly, during mass.

Mom drops her spoon on her plate. It makes a loud clank, a sound you would expect to hear coming from a restaurant kitchen. Graham, this really isn't funny.

It's not supposed to be funny, Mom. It's a miracle.

Dad leans back in his chair. He puts both hands on his belly, as if feeling it for ripeness. We were all at mass. How come we didn't notice Father Al flying? he says.

He didn't fly much. Just for a few seconds, and just barely off the ground.

Still, we would have noticed, Mom says.

Maybe the miracle was just for me, Graham says.

If only one person sees it, is it a miracle or a hallucination? Dad says.

Dear God, Help

In the same spot next to the bed, in the same position, Graham prays, again:

Dear God, help.

I need some direction. You showed me a miracle, but I'm not sure why. Why did you pick me to see Father Al fly? There must be a reason—I'm sure you don't make miracles just for the hell of it. In the Bible miracles are important, and they amaze people, and they change the way people think, and they make people believe and follow you. In the Bible miracles are powerful.

Not that your Father Al miracle wasn't powerful. It changed me, and it made me believe even more, but it seems like there should be something else. What am I not getting? What am I not understanding?

Help me, God. Or at least help me help myself. I've heard you like to do that, help people help themselves.

Amen.

Dear Father Al

Confessionals at St. Paul's require a choice. Walk in the door on the far left, and you'll sit down right across from the priest and give your confession face-to-face. He will be able to read your body language. He will be able to look you in the eye. Walk in the door to the right, and you're in a little room, separated from the priest by a yellowish screen that you can hear through but can't see through. Confession through the right door is anonymous. Graham chooses the right door. Graham always chooses the right door.

Graham walks in and kneels on the kneeler. It squeaks under his weight. The room is small, like a shower stall, and illuminated by a single odd bulb that fills the space with a dull orange light, light like the glow of a campfire reflected on the faces around it.

The confessional scared Graham when he first started going, back in the fourth grade. But it has not scared him for a while now. Graham now thinks confession is wonderful, if done right. In the confessional, you don't have to say all of your sins—imagine how long that would take. You just have to mention a few of the biggest sins, but when you walk out of confession, all of your sins are forgiven. This, thinks Graham, is a great deal.

Graham always picks his sins to say carefully and picks his words carefully when he feels he must say a serious sin. Graham thinks giving a good confession may be a little bit like being a good lawyer, because you have to be honest in the confessional, but you also want to find the best way to present your case. Graham plans to be a lawyer when he grows up.

But Graham knows today's confession will be different. Today, confession scares Graham.

Father Al clears his throat, loud. It sounds to Graham like Father Al is gargling marbles.

Graham starts, Bless me, Father, for I have sinned, and there's other things Graham is supposed to say—confession has a script, too—but, all of a sudden, Graham forgets the script. He squeezes his eyes shut and tries to remember what should come next, but he can't. Graham searches inside his own head for the next line of the script but finds only the five words that make this confession different and scary. So he blurts them out: Father, I saw a miracle.

What's that?

And then it all pours out of Graham. He is not picking his words at all. They seem to be picking him.

Graham says he was not doing a good job of paying attention to the homily on Sunday, and he is sorry about that. But, Graham says, he did pay attention to the sound of Father Al's footsteps when he walked away from the lectern, and Graham says he heard those footsteps stop. And then Graham tells Father Al about seeing him fly. Graham gives Father Al all the details about how high and how long he flew, about the light and air between his heavy black shoes and the floor.

Graham takes a deep breath. He wants to stop talking, but he does not.

Graham says, Father Al, the miracle was great, but it's also confusing me. I feel like I'm supposed to do something with the miracle, but I don't know what, and sometimes I'm scared that I didn't really see a miracle, that maybe it's just Satan playing tricks on me or maybe I'm just going plain old crazy, but then when I think these thoughts I get scared that I'm disappointing God, making him mad at me because he went and showed me a miracle, but I'm too stupid to understand it.

Then Graham's words stop, and he leans forward on the kneeler and rests the top of his head against the screen that hides him from Father Al. Graham does this because he feels very tired. He feels very tired because he feels empty.

Graham waits for Father Al.

And then Graham hears Father Al, softly but clearly, his snoring surprisingly melodic for a man who clears his throat like he is gargling marbles.

Flight

St. Paul's is empty when Graham walks out of the right door of the confessional, the lights are low, his footsteps the only sound. Each footstep starts like a slap as Graham walks towards the altar, the rubber of his sneaker sole striking the cold floor. But each slap echoes. The sound grows larger and larger, like it's rippling out and up, like maybe the sounds of Graham's footsteps are collecting in, are filling, the big vaulted ceiling.

Graham stops when he is near the center of the chancel, and he looks up. There hovers the big plaster Jesus, hanging from the wooden cross, arms outstretched, drops of blood near the crown of thorns on his head, near the nails driven through his palms. And he is looking down at Graham.

Then Graham jumps. Graham feels his feet leave the ground, feels them churn the air, feels them free, touching nothing.

Then SLAP, like a super footstep, a sound bigger than all of his other steps, a sound so big it just might fill up the whole church.

Then Graham jumps again, and his feet leave the ground, and he feels them churn the air and ripple the light inches above the floor, and he feels the plaster Jesus looking down on him, and, at least for that moment, that is enough.

Incandescence

There is some evidence that a carbide filament bulb burning in the Fire Department, Livermore, South Alameda County, California, has been burning since 1901.

--Guinness Book of World Records, 1978

The first one came to the firehouse hot on the heels of the black cables that suddenly ran across South Alameda County skies. The cables, sagging under the weight of curious crows, tied home to pole, home to pole, home to pole, one after another, knit the whole town together. Electricity was new and exciting then. The air crackled with the promise of a future brighter than ever imagined the night the first moonlight baby arrived.

*

There had been one baby earlier, a flesh baby, left on the firehouse steps the night before the electricity came on. The old timers say that baby was tow-headed with eyes the blue of cornflowers. They say she had chubby cheeks, a dimple in her chin. The old timers say the note pinned to her blanket just said *Pauline*, but the pink ribbon around her wrist carried a wavering, hand-embroidered promise: *I am going away, but remain close.*

*

The first moonlight baby arrived the night after the electricity came on.

Nobody saw how it got in, but there it was, belly down, elbows out, legs kicking as it pulled itself through the air, circling and circling the single glowing bulb hanging from the ceiling just inside the firehouse front door. The floating baby shone silver white, the color of moonlight on fresh snow, and when Chief Bob Gillespie followed its flight he could look right through the baby to rookie firefighter Glenn McKibben, his face bathed in silvery light, eyes wide, mouth open, as he stood across the room from Gillespie.

And then the light left McKibben's face and the baby was gone. Vanished. Just like that. Just like flipping a switch.

McKibben stared at Gillespie for a second before they each turned away from the other and exited the room in opposite directions, each feeling as if the room they were leaving was brighter, warmer than the room they had entered.

*

They grappled with flames, breathed heat and smoke, and they never flinched. But that very first baby, the flesh baby, brought them all to their knees. That's how the old timers always start when asked what the firefighters did with Pauline

There were six on duty that night, all sworn to protect, to risk their own lives to save others in need. They made a basinet out of a washtub and three wool blankets. They put Pauline in the tub, put the tub in the center of the big round table where they shared meals between fire runs and games of cribbage.

Gathered around the table, hovering over baby, they considered their options.

"No sense in looking for the mother. Not tonight. Maybe not ever."

"Could call the doc, but it's late, and what can he really do for her tonight?"

"Could take her to the hospital. She'd be safe there, cared for."

"She's safe here, cared for. It's just one night. Let her rest."

They stayed up that night to watch the baby, all six of them, together. Each man felt a loosening of his muscles, a growing warmth in his chest with each breath the sleeping baby took.

They cared for her the whole night. They cared for her until she was gone. They cared for her even after she was gone.

They didn't call it crib death then, the old timers say. They just called it gone.

*

Not even the old timers can say when exactly the moonlight babies' visits became a regular occurrence. Now the moonlight babies come like fireflies. They appear every night. Sometimes only two or three arrive. Other nights there are so many, moonlight babies rollicking like a pile of pups, a swirling fog of silvery legs and tiny hands and shining faces, moonlight babies impossible to count circling that simple firehouse bulb.

The firefighters let the old timers come and watch. They bring their own lawn chairs, pull them up against the walls. Better to not be too close to the light. Better to give the moonlight babies space to play.

*

The fate of the moonlight babies is a topic of much discussion. Each moonlight baby vanishes minutes after it appears. Some spectators say they hear a pop, a sound like a cork coming out of a bottle each time a moonlight baby disappears. Some say the sound is more like the flipping of a switch.

On the question of where the babies vanish to, there is no consensus.

Some say the moonlight babies just burn themselves out like fireworks, glow fierce and beautiful for one moment and are gone forever the next.

Others say nonsense. Others say look at the way the way the moonlight babies circle the bulb. They are light returning to light. The moonlight babies never disappear. They just join the light.

*

Every night the moonlight babies come to the firehouse, all sorts of them. Some roll; some crawl; a few toddle up on their toes, elbows in, hands flapping. Some hardly move at all, arrive flat on their backs, fingers occasionally grasping, reaching toward the firehouse light. Some moonlight babies share gummy smiles. Some moonlight babies flash rows of tiny teeth slick as pearls. Some of the babies are big and plump, thighs and arms like stacks of dinner rolls. Too many of the moonlight babies are stick thin.

But every moonlight baby arrives wearing a pink ribbon around its wrist. And every pink ribbon carries the same embroidered promise: *I am going away, but remain close.*

Lightning Woman Takes Three Lovers

The woman behind the Kroger bakery counter smells like sugar and sweat. She reads the top of the cake as she hands it to Caroline. "Banjo? That's an unusual nickname." Her faint blonde eyebrows rise and arch as she speaks.

"Yes, it is," Caroline says.

This isn't exactly a lie. Caroline agrees that Banjo is an odd nickname, just like Trumpet or Bassoon would be an odd nickname. However, in this case, Banjo is not a nickname at all. Banjo is the proper and only name of Caroline's beagle. But Caroline is too preoccupied to explain Banjo to the bakery woman.

Who will be my lightning lover? Who will be my lightning love? The ghost clinging to Caroline's back asks the same two questions over and over again, whispering them into Caroline's ear, the ghost's voice an electric hum tickling Caroline's neck even as she leans toward the counter to receive her cake.

1

Dave scooped the dirty clothes off his dorm room floor, piled them in his closet, shut the door. He burned sandalwood incense. He bought his roommate a pizza, a bribe to get him out of the room for a night. He asked Jackie from down the hall if he could borrow a condom. Jackie said, "Borrow? Just keep it. I don't want it back."

Dave and Caroline both knew. They hadn't talked about it. They didn't need to. After six months together, they shared the same thoughts, the way the chambers of the heart share the same blood, the way a pair of lungs shares breath. All of their individual ideas, desires, and fears had woven together into some unnamable thing that bound them one to the other.

Dave and Caroline shared the thought that the time had come and that this first time should be proper, should be sweet.

So Dave walked to Caroline's dorm. She stood outside waiting for him, just as he had asked her to. Watching him come toward her she felt her breath catch, like watching a fire suddenly bloom. Dave took her hand. They walked across campus to the auditorium, their fingers laced together. A cold March wind, heavy with the promise of rain, raised the downy hairs on the back of their necks.

They found seats in the fifth row. The lights dimmed, the music of the university orchestra filled the auditorium, filled Dave and Caroline. And they both felt it, a tingling washing across their skin, and as they sat back and leaned toward each other, they shared the thought *so this is what it feels like to be grown and sophisticated and in love.*

They didn't notice the grey sky and puddles as they walked back to Dave's dorm. They only noticed each other, the way their footsteps clicking against the cobblestones came together to make a sound like a tap dance, the way their right index fingers reached for the up button of the dorm elevator at the same moment, the way their weight made the end of Dave's bed sink, curl around them, coax them together as they sat next to each other. Their thighs touched, and each one felt the heat of the other.

They tried to talk about the music, about the boom of kettle drums and the way a violin can sound jaunty and heartbroken at the same time. But they quickly shared the thought *enough already, it's time.* And while they made love, Caroline looked up into Dave's eyes and saw herself reflected there, saw herself brand new.

The brown hair that hung down to her shoulders and bounced while she walked, gone. The face that looked so much like her mother's, gone. The thick shoulders and firm thighs earned through her years on the high school rowing team, gone. Skin and bones and muscles and organs and fluids, all of it, gone.

Finding her reflection in Dave's eyes Caroline saw a sparking yellow orb, bright and electric. A ball of thrumming light the size of a pumpkin. Caroline watched herself, revolving, quivering, floating. She tried to speak but only hissed, a sound like a pot starting to boil. She felt the absence of the weight of her body, felt raging heat at her center. She watched Dave's eyes grow big as fists, watched his mouth open, a silent scream. He rolled off of Caroline with all the haste and panic of a man dodging the snap of an alligator.

Making love to Dave, Caroline became ball lightning.

As quick as a thunderclap becomes a memory, plain Caroline returned. The hair, the face, the skin and bones and muscle, the organs and fluids, all back. Dave lay next to Caroline on the bed, but even as she listened to his breathing, deep and ragged, she felt a distance growing between them.

"What was that?" Dave asked.

"It felt wonderful."

"What was it?"

"Will you hold me?" Caroline asked.

And Dave said, "You feel like watching a movie?" which seemed an odd response from a man she shared thoughts with.

Caroline couldn't know then that when she had become ball lightning she had burnt up that unnamable thing that held her to Dave and Dave to her. Caroline couldn't know their shared thoughts had already started to unravel, to fray and drift apart like cottonwood fluff caught in a swirling wind. She couldn't know that those thoughts would continue to diverge, every second the gap between them growing until, only seven hours in the future, Caroline would look at Dave with watery eyes and say, "Please. Stay."

And Dave would say, "I gotta go."

*

Normally, Caroline would admire the cakes in the display case, most round, a few rectangular, white and yellow and pale blue and pink frosting, all of them pretty and sweet as prom dresses. But not today. Today the ghost on her back is cold and damp, makes her shiver. Today the ghost on her back won't stop. *Who will be my lightning lover? Who will be my lightning love?*

Caroline gets up on her toes, stretches her arms over the counter, accepts her cake from the Kroger bakery woman. It feels heavy in her hands, substantial, like a fat old Bible. White icing covered on top with a rainbow, swirls of marshmallow clouds, and in swooping red letters "Happy Birthday Banjo." A new thought appears, comes darting in on dragonfly wings to join the ghost's voice in Caroline's head. *This cake needs something.*

"Gonna be a big party?" the Kroger bakery woman asks.

Caroline opens her mouth to speak. All that comes out is a squeak.

The new thought is gone, maybe scared away. *Who will be my lightning lover? Who will be my lightning love?*

2

"Please. Stay," Caroline said.

The sound of Dave's boots pounding against the tile in the dorm hallway, echoing against the cinderblock walls of the stairwell, down, down, down, shook something loose inside of Caroline, made her feel anxious, off balance. She had to get out. As she walked to the library, she felt something cold and heavy settle into her chest.

She marched among the stacks, up one aisle, down the next, scanning the shelves rising high above her. It took almost an hour, but she found them, huddled together like a council of wise old women: *Essentials of Meteorology: An Invitation to the Atmosphere*; *Meteorology in America, 1800-1870*; *Introduction to Meteorology*; *Handbook of Meteorology*, and many, many more, hundreds of volumes, all promising to illuminate the mysteries of wind and water, the movement of waves, the bending of light, the blooming of electricity in the air.

Caroline let her right hand decide where to begin. She got up on her toes and pulled down two books from a shelf above her head. She piled them at her feet. She pulled three more to the left of her eye level, several more to her right, added them to her pile. She squatted and plucked books from the bottom shelf. The voids she left formed the points of a cross, and as Caroline knelt to force her hands under the tower of books, she looked like a believer praying.

Stooped, her chin resting on *Advances in Meteorology and Hydrology*, Caroline carried her collection of books to a nearby table. The corners of their covers poked her ribs and stomach. The pile tipped as she set it down, the falling books spilling across the tabletop, a quick succession of muffled thuds, a sound like an echo of Dave's fleeing footsteps.

Caroline bent to pick up the single volume that had dropped to the floor. It smelled like mildew and pipe smoke when she opened it. She flipped past the title and copyright pages, found the table of contents and scanned, running her finger down the page as if she might be able to recognize what she searched for by touch, as if she might feel it, electricity thrumming against the pad of her fingertip. She scanned and flipped and scanned and flipped. Meteorology terminology, as slick and elusive as mercury, flowed under her finger. But what she needed wasn't there. She turned the book over, opened the back cover, thumbed hurriedly through the final pages, a sound like shuffling cards. This is what mattered now, beginnings and endings. She found the *L*s in the index, ran her finger along the tiny print, but it wasn't there. She turned more pages, found the *B*s. It wasn't there either. She set the book on the floor, picked another off the table, opened it, raised a finger in the air, ready to scan and flip.

For thirty straight nights Caroline returned to her library table, gathering new piles of books, discarding those that didn't mention ball lightning, devouring the few that did. Passages on the long history of reports of ball lightning made the cold and heavy thing in her chest throb. Notes on how science could not reproduce it in a lab made the cold and heavy thing expand.

On her thirtieth night in the library, she was reading a passage that made the cold and heavy thing in her chest throb when she felt a hand on her shoulder. She turned to look. Jackie.

"Are you okay? You look kind of frazzled."

"I guess I have felt better."

"Do you want to take a break? Go for a walk?"

"Yes, I do," Caroline said, her voice as sharp and sure as the crack of a gavel.

It happened the way Caroline had always suspected such things happened.

They went back to Jackie's room.

They drank cheap beers Jackie found in the back of his roommate's mini fridge.

They pretended to explore the profundities of love and loss.

"I feel like a part of me has been ripped away," Caroline said.

"Love is a wild ride," Jackie said.

"So wild."

Caroline leaned in toward Jackie, pretended she found comfort in his words, pretended she could weave his clichés into something she could wrap herself in, warm and safe. And Jackie pretended that's what he wanted to do, to find the words, the incantation, to warm and protect Caroline.

They played their roles long enough that if either of them told the story in the future they could say *I'm not sure what happened; we were just talking and one thing led to another, and the next thing you know.*

While they made love, Caroline climbed on top of Jackie, pinned his shoulders to the mattress. She looked down at Jackie, his face pinched shut like a man caught in a spotlight.

"Look at me," Caroline said.

And Jackie opened his eyes, and there she was, reflected in Jackie's watery pupils. Shimmering, sparking, all yellow glow and radiant heat, Caroline was ball lightning.

Jackie croaked, "What's happening?" and cringed beneath Caroline, but Caroline did not hear him.

Caroline heard herself hissing and crackling. She felt the heat and energy at her center. She felt Jackie, so frail, wilting in the presence of that heat. She felt the cold heavy thing that lived in her chest circling her, promising a quick return.

*

"Is something wrong?" the Kroger bakery woman asks.

Caroline looks up from the cake. Furrows crease the bakery woman's brow. Her eyes are bright as a comet's flash. *Who will be my lightning lover? Who will be my lightning love?*

"I'm sorry. I just think it's missing something," Caroline says.

"I know just the thing."

Who will be my lightning lover?

And the Kroger bakery woman reaches across the counter to take back the cake. Her arms tense only slightly, ready and accepting.

3

Enveloped in the still, humid air of a confessional, Caroline spoke to a wall separating her from a priest she had never met. She felt the thing in her chest vibrating as she started to speak. "Bless me, Father, for I have sinned. It has been many years since my last confession. I come to you today seeking penance and reconciliation. Seven years ago, I took two lovers. Since then, though I try and try, I have not slept through the night. Since then, every night, impure images of these men haunt my sleep."

Caroline's confession, a cocktail of truth and lies.

Truth: Seven years had passed since her lone night with Jackie.

Truth: Since making love to Jackie, Caroline had never slept through the night.

Truth: Vivid images startled Caroline awake every night.

Lie: Images of Dave and Jackie were not her tormentors. Dave and Jackie appeared only as part of the background, no more significant than the empty beer cans, the rumple of sheets kicked to the floor. Caroline's specter, instead, images of herself as ball lightning.

Lie: For two weeks, Caroline had not tried to sleep. She closed her eyes each night anxious for the arrival of her visions, the chance to study herself as ball lightning. When she concentrated hard enough, she could see yellow light pushing back the shadows of her bedroom, feel warmth against her cheeks.

"But that's all you've experienced for seven years, just impure thoughts? No actions?" The priest's voice sounded like the rustle of dry leaves.

"Just thoughts," Caroline said. The truth.

"I understand," said the priest. One hundred percent lie, a complete impossibility.

How could a faceless priest understand the ecstasy of becoming light and energy, the fear that ecstasy would never be felt again? How could he understand the pain of confronting the fragility of partners? Had he spent years carry something cold and heavy in his chest?

How could he understand the relentless search for understanding? Had he read every meteorology book in the university library? Had he taken the same Intro to Earth Science course at the community college three times? How many hours had he studied the skies trying to will the air to spark?

Did the faceless priest feel envy and lust when thunderstorms bloomed across his windows? Had he taken home a beagle from the pound, just to have a companion to ride out those storms? Did he look at every person who crossed his path with suspicion and hope, wondering if they understood, wondering if they had been ball lightning, if they had loved ball lightning. Did he inspect their pupils, their skin, alert for a yellow glow? Did he wonder if a beagle could be trained to sniff the air around strangers, bark at traces of sulfur?

Did the priest understand what it felt like when after seven years something cold and heavy in your chest starts to change, to become something lighter than air, maybe a vapor, a gas? Did he understand what it felt like to sit in a confessional and realize you're really talking to yourself. Caroline understood. She gave herself over to the thing in her chest, let it lift her right out of her seat. She floated out of the confessional before the faceless priest could deliver her penance, floated out of the church, floated across the church parking lot. She floated right into her car.

Caroline sat in her car, hovering just above the driver's seat, and felt the thing that had been inside of her for so long, making its way outside of her. It seeped out of her pores, collected like fog on the floor of the car, rose up before her, gray and cold, but unmistakable, a friend returning.

As Caroline drove to Kroger to pick up a cake for her beagle's birthday party, the ghost of Caroline as ball lightning rode shotgun, whispering the whole time *Who will my lightning lover? Who will be my lightning love?*

*

The bakery woman returns to the counter, Caroline's cake in her hands. She tilts the edge of the cake closet to her chest up toward her chin. "How's that look?" she asks.

Who will be my lightning love?

In the arch of the rainbow, a thick round blob of yellow icing throws off a tight shower of yellow dots.

"Is that. . .?" says Caroline.

"Ball lightning," says the bakery woman. "Have you heard of it? Spectacular. One of nature's mysteries. For hundreds of years people have reported seeing it. Yet the scientists all say they can't prove it exists."

"Have you seen it?"

"Many times."

"How do you feel about birthday parties for dogs?"

"They are my favorite occasions."

And the ghost on Caroline's back starts to vibrate and hum. A yellow glow fills the Kroger bakery, a blooming of sparks. Heat and light ripple through Caroline's center, spread toward the top of her head, the tip of her toes. Heat and light spread everywhere.

Holding Sampson

Sampson was an accident, a product of a fused blossom, probably, and storm water reaching more roots than leaves, of unusually hot, sunny days and unseasonably crisp nights. Nature, not science, not any human hands, birthed Sampson. Claire called it a miracle. Claire might have been right.

Among the six scraggly plants we had growing in our single bed along the garage, Sampson stood out like a diamond in a coal bin even early on. While the other tomatoes looked like green acorns emerging from the vines, Sampson already looked like a green fist, the punch of a monster. "Well, look at that," Claire said nodding toward green Sampson as we worked side-by-side weeding our small patch.

"Ain't that somthin'," I said, and reached toward green Sampson just as Claire reached for green Sampson, our hands moving parallel to each other, as if we were each a funhouse mirror for the other, as if the same need had been born in each of us at the exact same moment.

It felt good, moving together, just Claire and me. That's how it had always been, just Claire and me. No kids. Not for lack of trying. Not for lack of heartbreak. But Claire and I didn't move together as much as we used to. Maybe that's just what fifty-odd years of marriage do to people. All the little slights and hurt feelings, the I-forgots and the never-noticings, the noticing-but-not-saying-thank-yous, maybe those all accumulate over the years and gum up the works like tar in a transmission. Maybe that buildup bogs down the whirring gears of love.

*

As days lengthened then receded, tomatoes grew. From green to pink to red they went, growing fat on sunshine and rain, their flesh

56

like a good handshake, warm and firm. And still Sampson put the other tomatoes to shame. One day he was three times their size, the next day five, the next maybe eight, maybe ten. We worried he'd be too much for the vine, so Claire built a hammock out of old pantyhose and cut-and-twisted wire hangers, something to take the weight off the vine, something to keep Sampson out of the dirt.

"How big do you think he'll get?" Claire asked me as June faded into July.

"As big as he wants, looks like."

*

The others were easy. He's a pretty red. Pick 'im. That one too, red as a cardinal. Pick 'im, and that one, and that one. We'd stretch the bottoms of our t-shirts into makeshift baskets and fill them with tomatoes for dinner. Extras Claire would ask me to take to the neighbors, but I'd always forget, so she would have to do it. She'd wander down the block, leaving tomatoes on porch railings, in mailboxes, anonymous kindness. But when do you pick a giant tomato? How do you know when it's become as big as it wants to be? Claire and I wore this conundrum like wet sweaters, questions heavy and irritating and impossible to ignore. Evenings, I'd crouch on my hands and knees in the dirt, one ear pressed to Sampson while Claire stood over me, her face pinched in thought. I'd flick my index finger against Sampson two times, three, four, five. "Stop," Claire would say. Six flicks. Seven. He'd make a sound like a tennis ball meeting concrete.

"I don't know," I'd say.

"Maybe one more day?"

"Yeah. One more day," I'd say. Claire would offer me a hand up. I'd refuse her help. Man pride. My bones would groan as I stood. And the next evening my knees would be back in the damp soil of our small garden plot, and in the cool of Claire's shadow I'd flick Sampson, bigger and redder than he had been the night before.

*

The dream was just a voice blooming in my head at three a.m., a rumbling in the night-black atmosphere still thick with summer humidity. The voice sounded like Charlton Heston, but it wasn't Charlton Heston. I recognized the voice from its first note the way some people recognize bird songs.

The voice said, "I'm as big as I want to be."

The voice said, "Now."

Claire was already in the garden when I arrived. She stood next to Sampson, the soft soil of the garden bed filling the gaps between her bare toes. "You heard it too," she said. Claire did the honors. No ceremony, just a quick tug. Just like that it was done. And just like that it had begun.

We walked back to the house side by side, Sampson riding in the basket of Claire's raised nightgown, our bare feet padding like cats' paws across the backyard grass.

*

The newspaperman appeared to be part cricket. His black hair was slicked back with pomade. He had beady, dark eyes. He hopped around the kitchen, chirping about finding the best light, chirping questions: "What variety? Grown from seed? How long? Any more?" The camera hanging from his neck swung along with his movements.

The morning after we picked Sampson we weighed him. While Claire brewed coffee and scrambled eggs in the kitchen, I rummaged around in the garage until I unearthed the old grocery scale Claire had bought at a flea market many years ago for reasons neither one of us could recall. Sampson looked regal sitting in the chrome basket of the scale, like an emperor in a polished chariot. Ten pounds, eight ounces. This was big, call-the-newspaper big.

The newspaperman scooped Sampson up from the table and put him on the counter then picked him back up again. He hopped in a tight little circle. "Fertilizer? Secrets?" He picked Sampson up. He put Sampson down. He waved his hands at me like a man trying to pluck dandelion fluff from the air. "Would you mind getting up? Stand behind the tomato. Thanks. There you go. Great. Oh. You too, Claire. It's Claire, right? Yep. That's it. Great. The loving couple behind the amazing tomato. That's the story. Just great. Perfect. Maybe not. Try picking the tomato up." I scooped Sampson up in both hands, presenting him to the camera like a priest making an offering. I felt his weight in my forearms, in my wrists. "That's better. Maybe. Claire? Claire, right? Get in there too, Claire."

Claire squeezed in closer. Her left shoulder leaned into my right shoulder, the way it used to when we walked through winter winds, Claire searching for warmth, me hoping my heat was enough. I felt her hand skittering under mine, looking for a hold on Sampson. I let my right hand fall away. Claire's hand moved in to take its place. My load lightened. I felt Sampson's warmth against my palm. I felt Claire's breath against my neck. Claire shifted her hand. Our fingers touched. I felt movement in my palm. At first I thought it was my pulse, my heartbeat. Then I realized it was coming from Sampson. Ba-dum, Ba-dum, Ba-dum. I felt it in my palm, steady and regular as a marching cadence. Ba-dum. Ba-dum. It matched my heartbeat. I felt Claire breathing next to me. In and out, in and out, the tickle of air against my neck, a feeling like electricity, electricity sparking in perfect time with my heartbeat, in perfect time with Sampson. "Do you feel it?" Claire whispered.

I mouthed *I do.*

"That's it. Perfect. Now smile. Perfect. Don't move."

We stood still, but even bathed in the white light of the camera's flash we never stopped moving. Breath and pulse and heartbeats, moving, me and Claire and Sampson, all moving together.

*

It's hard to say exactly how it started. Maybe it started right after the newspaperman left and I pulled Claire to me, my right hand resting on the small of Claire's back, Claire's fingertips skipping along my left forearm, tongues of fire blooming in our eyes. Or maybe it started earlier. Maybe it started with the flash of the newspaperman's camera or with the tug that freed Sampson from the vine, or maybe it started with the planting of a seed, an act of hope and faith. Or maybe it started many, many years ago with the first joke Claire ever told me, the first time we laughed together.

I can say how it ended: Claire and I sweaty and naked on the kitchen floor, our limbs jumbled together like a game of pick-up-sticks, my arms and legs, hollow, numb, electricity crackling in my chest.

As soon as the newspaper man left, Claire and I made love on the kitchen floor. Mouth on mouth, tongue on tongue, the sharing of breath, we took our time. When we finished, I stayed on the kitchen floor, tangled with Claire, and watched the slow rising and falling of her chest as she drifted off to sleep.

*

Amazing read the caption below our picture in the paper the next day. It's a good picture, black and white. Claire wears her white hair like a crown of clouds. My eyes sparkle, black as shale. Sampson, a slick grey, steadfast and pretty as polished steel, claims the foreground. It's an amazing picture.

Amazing said the neighbors who came to the house asking to see Sampson. Some asked the same questions the newspaperman had: Variety? Fertilizer? Secrets? Some talked weather and sports. They all told stories about their tomatoes, how they had once, not too far back, grown one almost as big as Sampson, maybe bigger, how they and their tomato probably should have been in the newspaper, too. They all said Sampson was amazing. And every night, when the people had all gone home, Claire and I made love on the kitchen floor. And every night before we fell asleep on that floor, curled together like a couple of pups, we'd look at each other and say together "Amazing," a word shared, a prayer of thanks.

*

The kitchen remained crowded even after the neighbors stopped coming by. Sampson took up some space, and me and Claire, of course, and stray dirty dishes lingering in the sink. Memories of having spent the last four nights making love to Claire in the kitchen filled every other square inch. Naked bodies dappled in moonlight and shadow. Sampson vibrating on the table. Claire's heart beating against my chest. Claire's touch clung to me like pine tar; I could not remove it from my skin. The memories swirled around me, everywhere, a flock of ghosts whispering lyrics to old love songs.

*

"Do you see it?" Claire said when she brought me my coffee. I sat in my chair at the kitchen table. Sampson, perched on a silver tray, sat in the center of the table, as dignified as a Thanksgiving turkey.

I stared at Sampson. "He's different," I said. Claire sat down across from me, and we both stared at Sampson, a pair of gypsies exploring a crystal ball.

"Different. But how?" Claire leaned in toward Sampson.

I reached out and touched Sampson. His flesh gave where it did not give before, a feeling like touching a package of raw meat. I waited for it, waited. The ghosts swirling around me stilled, shushed each other quiet. Finally, it came, fainter, maybe slower than before, but it was still there, vibrations in my fingertips. Ba. Dum. "He's dying," I said.

"I guess we always knew this would come."

We both knew what we would do next. We both knew we didn't have a choice.

*

It was about Sampson. It was about letting Sampson be Sampson. It was about respect. It was about thanks.

We started by moving Sampson and his silver platter to the kitchen counter, higher ground, closer to God. Claire and I took up positions behind the counter. Shoulder to shoulder, we looked down upon Sampson's failing red flesh. Claire took my right hand in her left. Electricity. I turned to look at Claire. Claire turned to look at me. She nodded. The ghosts of our love making quieted, swallowed their lyrics about red roses and true hearts and blue dreams of yesterday, swallowed all their I-can't-stops and their I do-do-dos. I lowered my head, retreated to the silence of my skull, waited for the right words to come to me.

I raised my eyes toward Sampson. I felt his vibration, his hum, weaker still, felt it moving down the counter, through the floorboards and nesting in the bottom of my feet. I spoke: "Amazing." Claire's hand tightened around mine.

I tipped my head back, looked at the ceiling. "Amazing." Louder this time, more bass. The dirty dishes in the sink rattled.

I squeezed Claire's hand and raised my arm, raised both of our arms. I looked to Claire. She looked to me. "Amazing," I said. The ghosts of our lovemaking ceased their swirling, drifted into tight rows behind Claire and I. Claire mouthed a word to me. I think she mouthed *more*. Sampson deserved more. We all deserved more.

"Amazing grace," I said, "How sweet the sound."

Claire joined in with me, her voice like caramel, rich and smooth. "That saved a wretch like me," we said together. We kept our joined hands in the air. We swayed side-to-side, slow, easy, together.

"I once was lost, but now I'm found." The ghosts of our lovemaking joined in, a chorus of whispers floating under our voices, "was blind but now I see." That was as much as I knew, so I took a deep breath and circled back to the start.

"Amazing." I punched the word, let it out like a command, and everybody stayed right with me. Me, Claire, the ghosts, note for note, breath for breath, together, "grace how sweet the sound that saved a wretch like me." We went through the whole thing three times. And then we stopped.

With my free hand I pulled a knife from the dish drainer. I grabbed the good knife, the one Claire was sensitive about me using, the one that sliced bread so thin you could read your newspaper through it. I passed the knife to my right hand. Together, Claire and I took up the knife and raised it above our heads. A burst of sunlight reflected off the blade, twinkled above Sampson like his very own star. The ghost chorus whispered behind us: "Amazing grace, how sweet the sound. . ." The vibrations in the soles of my feet stilled.

A nod to Claire was all it took. The cut was guillotine quick, clean as surgery. A disk of Sampson's flesh, slick with seeds and juice, lay on the tray. The ghosts whispered on: "I once was lost, but now I'm found." Together Claire and I cut the slice of Sampson in half. Together we lay the good knife on the tray next to Sampson. Separately we each picked up half of the slice. Together we entwined our arms. Together each fed the other. Tomato seeds, slick as quicksilver, dribbled down our chins.

*

Claire and I spent the rest of the morning eating Sampson. Most of the ghosts of our love making retreated. They moved into the cabinets we seldom opened, they moved under the refrigerator. One disappeared down the sink drain. Many of them receded right into the walls, ghosts joining plaster and lathe. But a few of the ghosts joined us at the kitchen table, kept us company while we finished Sampson. They whispered while we ate.

They whispered the first joke Claire ever told me, many, many years ago: "Why didn't the skeleton go to the dance? Because he didn't have any body to dance with."

They whispered a joke I would tell Claire months in the future in a dimly lit hospital room: "How does the ocean say goodbye? It doesn't. It just waves." The last joke I would ever tell Claire.

But mostly, they whispered "Amazing." Claire and I filled our mouths with the goodness of tomato, flesh and seeds and juice, while those ghosts whispered, "Amazing," over and over and over again.

Hot Dog Queen

Frankfurters.

23 (2-ounce) in 3 minutes 10
seconds by Linda K____, 21, at
Veterans Stadium, Philadelphia on
July 12, 1977.

--Guinness Book of World Records, 1978

The thing that lives inside of me has milky grey eyes blind as beans.

They are warm and damp and clammy, the hotdogs in my hands. They feel like a feverish child's forehead. They smell like a humid July afternoon, clouds building, flesh sticky with sweat. Strawberry-blonde hairs on my forearms, baby soft and fine, tingle, rise. Every eye in Veterans Stadium crawls along my skin.

The thing inside of me has a mouth full of knives, sharp steel where teeth should be.

They've put me in the middle, lined us up near home plate boy, boy, boy, girl, boy, boy, boy. I feel the presence of the men surrounding me. Their anger and their fear, the hunger they have cultivated for this moment, it all wafts off of them like pheromones. It crackles like sparklers, charges the air, a hazy glow. They breath slow and heavy. They anticipate.

The thing has a mouth like a garbage disposal, a chaos of blades, swirling and frantic as a flock of sparrows caught in a tiny glass room.

I stand in the ravine between two giant men. They've put the biggest ones next to me, one to my left, one to my right. This is not an accident. It's an old carny trick, playing with perspective. The human eye is gullible, easy to manipulate. Standing between the two biggest men I am trapped in a spotlight, exposed. Standing next to the giants I am a little girl come to play among the redwoods. Standing next to the giant men I am so, so small.

The thing inside me is part cotton candy machine. It breathes warm, sugary breath. I taste it in my throat, feel it, anxious puffs against the inside of my skin.

The men to my right and left have bellies like truck tires, chests like beer kegs. Their forearms are baked hams, their faces beaten dough. The big men's wide shadows are neon signs proclaiming, "Look. She's a woman. A small, small woman."

The thing inside me is part railroad train.

Once the buzzer sounds, momentum takes over. While my left hand rises, brings a hot dog to my mouth, my right falls down to the table, skitters like a spider among the dogs, finds its grip. When my right hand rises, fingers curled around a hot dog, the left hand falls. A rhythm, unbroken, familiar, perfect—*Click-clack, Click-clack*. It rattles through my bones.

The thing is part vacuum cleaner.

When a hot dog nears my mouth it starts to vibrate. There it is, a twinge in the soft pads of my fingertips, and then the hot dog flies, hovers between my hand and my mouth. For just an instant, each hot dog rides the air as steady and beautiful as a dragonfly.

The thing is part street-corner messiah.

The thing calls and the hot dogs follow. They zip into my mouth, zip down my throat, determined. As single-minded as kisses, they race into the darkness.

The thing is part black hole.

*

Strangers will question me after I've shamed the big men, after I've won: Where did you put them all? Are you okay? How does it feel, so many hot dogs? The truth is it feels like breathing, essential. I will tell people I just love to eat. I will tell people there's just something inside of me; I have never been full. This is also the truth. We just want to feel full.

The thing is part forest fire.

Hot dog #1 is an ancient maple, sap boiling to the surface, sticky and alive. Hot dog #2 an evergreen brushing the clouds, pinecones hiss and pop. Hot dog #7 a young ash, gnarled bark throbbing an orange glow. Hot dog #15 a tangle of crawling weeds twisting in the heat. Hot dog #22 an oak, trunk wider than a big man's hug, canopy lit up like Vegas. Everything a dance of flames. Everything light and heat. Everything racing toward ashes.

The thing inside of me is heartbroken.

The thing inside of me is dog loyal.

Hot dog #23 disappears into the thing. We nurture each other as best we know how. Philadelphia watches and cheers like an approaching storm.

Loving Providers

Dear Ted and Judy,

While I must admit that any mail I get here is exciting, I want you to know I was especially pleased to hear from you. Who would have guessed that after all these years it would be a blurb in the alumni magazine that brought us back together? I wish they would have used a better picture of me.

Congrats on the success of the dealership. It sounds as if you have been truly blessed. I can't say this comes as a shock. Looking back on our college days, even then it was clear you both had a special relationship with Christ. You practically glowed with his love. Ford is lucky to have you.

In your letter, you asked for more details about my work. Well, I've been in Chad for a little over a year now and plan on staying as long as the Lord needs me here. As for day-to-day things, yes, it's really hot, and, yes, I eat strange things occasionally (bats, bugs, the head of a goat), but, basically, things are good. My main project right now is the orphanage. Currently, we are taking care of twelve children, four boys and eight girls. Many days things get a little rough around here, but the satisfaction of knowing I'm doing God's work more than makes up for the disappointments and frustrations.

Excuse me for rushing into business, but the generator is starting to chug the way it does when it's nearly out of fuel, so I'm trying to finish this before the lights go out. Yes, we surely could use your support. Right now, I'm in the process of trying to find sponsors for each of the children. Basically, this would entail you sending a check periodically. That money would go towards supporting a particular child.

Then, every so often, I would send you an update on the child so you could see the difference your donations make. As I said, I've just begun working on this, so, if you're interested, you could be the first to join this project. You would be providing me the opportunity to test the process, and together we could put God's love into action.

Please prayerfully consider this exciting opportunity to make a difference in a child's life and let me know what you think.

In Christ's Peace,
Bill

Dear Ted and Judy,

Your first check arrived yesterday. May God bless you both. Truly, this feels like manna from heaven. Your contribution may seem small to you, but, trust me, it will change lives in Chad. I firmly believe that this new venture will transform children's futures and serve as a tool to spread God's message.

Let me tell you about the child that your money will be supporting. Her name is Nemerci, and she was one of the very first children to arrive at the orphanage. We believe Nemerci is around eight years old. She is a quiet little girl with a wiry frame, big eyes, and a cautious smile. She is often shy around the other children, but is an extremely good worker, always willing to help in the kitchen or sweep the grounds or fetch water from the well. I chose Nemerci because I thought your support might be just the thing she needs to gain a bit more self-confidence. I assure you that, while she is shy, she is very bright and possesses a strong faith.

I have to run to Bible study, but let me thank you once again for your generosity. I hope you enjoy the enclosed picture of Nemerci. Please don't be startled by her swollen belly. I promise you it doesn't slow her down at all.

I'll write again soon and let you know how things are progressing.

In Christ's Peace,

Bill

P.S. I still need a catchy name for this project and a title for your role. Others here think you should be called "sponsors," but that seems awfully cold to me. Let me know if you have ideas.

Dear Ted and Judy,

Ban wa? That means *How are you?* in Ngumbaye. I'm taking lessons from a local schoolteacher. I hope learning the language will help me to run things around here a little more efficiently. I have the hardest time communicating with the groundskeeper and the cook.

I must say that I was surprised by your last check. I thought we had agreed on an amount far less than this, but I'm thrilled by your enthusiasm. I followed all of your instructions, and I'm pleased to report that Nemerci is fine. I had her examined by a French doctor, who works in a city about twenty miles from here. It turns out that she had a slight case of kwashiorkor, but, thanks to your support, I've been able to add more protein to her diet, and she already seems to be gaining new vigor. The other night I even saw her playfully snatch peanuts from a smaller child. Miracles really do happen every day. Nemerci asked me to thank you and wants to know if you could send a picture of yourselves.

Thank you for your ideas about titles. We have decided to name the project "Hope to One, Hope to All," and we will be calling those who donate "Loving Providers," as you suggested. You are still our only Loving Providers, but I expect this will give us the opportunity to work out any bugs before expanding the program.

Thanks again for your thoughtful support. You really are making a difference. I'll write again soon. I've enclosed a picture of the new and improved Nemerci.

In Christ's Peace,
Bill

Dear Loving Providers Ted and Judy,

Greetings from Hope to One, Hope to All. Here in Southern Chad, the hot season has begun. This is a tough time of year, with temperatures climbing above one hundred degrees most days. But, so long as God is willing, we expect our food supply will hold out until he brings the rains and the villagers are able to begin planting.

Your package arrived last week. Nemerci jumped with excitement when she got it. She loves the dress. At first she was scared to wear it. I imagine she worried about ruining it, but one of the women in the kitchen convinced her to put it on. The red looks brilliant against her dark skin.

Nemerci, our once shy little girl, has become the talk of the compound. All of the children and many of the villagers are impressed with her new clothes and are paying her a great deal of attention, and she is blossoming. She's developed new confidence and is even becoming a leader among the children. Sadly, several of them seem to resent her new status, and I've even seen this resentment lead to blows once or twice. But Nemerci has been eating well and, having beaten the kwashiorkor, grows stronger every day. Truly, the Lord walks with her. Just the other day I saw her reduce a nine-year-old boy to tears after he tried to grab her dress. She has a right hook like a stinger missile. The Lord works in mysterious ways when protecting the littlest lambs of his flock.

Thanks again for your continued support. Nemerci and I are keeping you in our prayers. I've enclosed a picture of Nemerci wearing the dress you sent.

In Christ's Peace,
Bill

Dear Loving Providers Ted and Judy,
Greetings from Hope to One, Hope to All. I expect that this letter comes as something of a surprise since I usually wait to write until after I have received your check, but after some intense praying, I feel certain that God is calling me to contact you.

It saddens me to report that we have run into some problems with Nemerci. I'll get right to the point. As I mentioned in the last letter, we are currently going through the hot season and must survive on a limited food supply until the rains come. I'm afraid that we are encountering some difficulties. The cook tells me that Nemerci has been eating more than her fair share.

The children all eat from a communal bowl, so meals have always been sort of catch-as-catch-can, and before the Lord brought you into Nemerci's life, I suspect that she often came out on the short end of the stick, but as of late, she has been dominating the children's meals. The cook, who is prone to exaggeration, tells me that Nemerci has been eating almost a third of the food that is meant to feed the twelve children. While I'm sure that the problem is not this severe, it is an issue that we must address. I have heard several of the smaller children crying themselves to sleep at night, crying from hunger, I fear.

Several people have talked to Nemerci about the problem, but it has had no effect on her. I guess you can't blame a hungry child for eating, but I worry that real trouble could develop if this continues. I hate to ask you this because you have been so generous already, but I have prayed long and hard, and the only solution I can see is the most obvious. I must ask you, our Loving Providers, if you would prayerfully consider slightly increasing the amount of your regular donation.

I have already made contact with a merchant who will sell us extra grain. Because food is scarce everywhere right now, his price is high, but once things start to grow again prices will come down, and you should be able to go back to making a smaller regular donation. Let me know how you feel about this or if you have any other suggestions.

While we have had these problems, God has certainly not abandoned us. I feel his presence and see his handiwork every day. Nemerci continues to flourish. Quite frankly, she has grown into one of the strongest, most-lively children I have seen in the region. Her wiry frame has filled out amazingly. The muscles in her shoulders and back ripple the fabric of her beautiful red dress as she works around the compound. She asked me to pass along her best wishes and asked if you would be sending any more gifts.

If you are unable to increase your donation, just let me know. I assure you that I will understand, and we will continue to do our best to provide for Nemerci and the rest of the children. I ask that you keep us all in your prayers.

In Christ's Peace,
Bill

Dear Loving Providers Ted and Judy,

Once again I find myself overwhelmed by your generosity. I received your check and the new larger dress yesterday. The fabric is stunning, as airy and smooth as spider webs.

I wish that I had good news to report, but I'm afraid that things here have not gotten any better. However, I'm sure that your financial support and prayers will go a long way towards improving the situation.

The new dress couldn't have come at a better time. The one that you sent earlier no longer fit, and Nemerci was refusing to wear any of the clothes available in the village market. I must tell you, this situation was getting quite embarrassing for all involved.

We were down to our last bag of grain when your check arrived. We should have had enough to last for several more months. Only the Lord knows where it all went, but I have suspicions that some of the villagers working at the center have been stealing from our storehouse. I questioned several of them, and they all fingered Nemerci, made wild claims about finding her rummaging in the granary late at night and such.

While I'm sure Nemerci didn't single handily decimate our supplies, she does continue to eat an alarming amount. I've used the money that you sent to purchase a great deal of millet, and I have increased Nemerci's daily ration of food. She no longer eats with the other children because mealtimes were becoming a sort of battle royale. Instead, she is served her meals separately. She seems to prefer this arrangement. I would have been able to purchase more grain, but I felt Christ calling me to hire a second cook. Of late, our original cook has been struggling. She claims that trying to keep Nemerci satisfied has made her workload unmanageable. I have had such a time with the help lately. God bless them.

After you have done so much, I find it very troubling to mention this, but, once again, I find that I must ask for your assistance. Paying for the second cook will be an ongoing expense not accounted for in the budget. I see no other way to meet Nemerci's needs, but if this is to continue, I'll need you to increase your already generous donation. Rest assured that your selfless giving is appreciated by everyone at Hope to One, Hope to All.

Nemerci asked me to be sure to say hello and to let you know she is praying for you. I've enclosed a picture of her in the new dress. See how strong she has become? Jesus' little warrior.

In Christ's Peace,
Bill

Dear Loving Providers Ted and Judy,

I have the unfortunate duty to deliver terrible news. Nemerci is gone. She disappeared several days ago. One of our staff members reported that three days ago when she called the children for breakfast Nemerci was nowhere to be found. Everyone here at Hope to One, Hope to All has been praying around the clock for Nemerci to return and doing everything possible to locate her, but, as of yet, we have not found her. To make matters worse, something has been getting into the village fields and ravaging the crops that have just started to grow. Some of the villagers believe that Nemerci is responsible for this. I have tried to reason with them, to explain that it must be wildlife destroying the crops, but no one listens to me. I have also heard reports of goats coming up missing. I can't guarantee Nemerci's safety if she is found by the villagers. They are quite upset. Nemerci desperately needs your prayers at this time.

It's imperative that the staff of Hope to One, Hope to All locate Nemerci before any of the villagers do. Mounting a full-scale search will be quite costly. We'll have to hire more trucks and drivers and, hopefully, a helicopter and pilot. There will be equipment to buy, binoculars and infrared cameras, new Bibles for those leading the prayer vigils.

We thank you, our dearest Loving Providers, in advance for your additional support during this crisis. I assure you we will launch our grand search for Nemerci the second your check arrives.

In Christ's Peace,
Bill

P.S. Hurry, please. For Nemerci.

The Mulberry Tree

Before you can hold starlight, you have to spend a thousand hours spinning on your back. This is something I learned by accident many years ago, when I was only fourteen. But I should slow down.

Before you can understand my starlight, you must know my tree, and in order to understand my tree, you must first know my father.

My father had one son. Me. My father liked this idea, the idea he had a son. He just wished that I wasn't that son. He never said this aloud. He didn't have to. This wish rippled out of his core, coming at me in waves. He'd roll his eyes when I spoke, his head slightly cocked, shaking, slowly, involuntarily, no, no, no. Those head shakes pushed up against me constantly, a tide to battle, pushing me away, away, away. Every night I fell to sleep with my arms and legs tingling, numbed by fatigue.

I don't blame my father for his wishes and his waves. He didn't choose them. I'm certain they were innate parts of him, same as his breath and bones. Back then I believed the wishes and the waves were my challenges to deal with, not his. I believed I had to become stronger than the waves. This is why I needed my tree.

My tree is a mulberry. An accident tree that nobody planted. It just showed up one day, a volunteer. And when it was young it was so small and so plain nobody noticed it. My father and I didn't notice the mulberry until it became a nuisance, its pale brown trunk thicker than my father's arm by then, its hundreds of spindly branches and thousands of bright green leaves dancing in every breeze, casting long, rippling shadows over the bed of peonies my mother planted before she died. Every so often my father would say, "We should take down that mulberry."

But taking down the mulberry required time and sweat, in combination, a cocktail my father could not craft. And so the mulberry grew and grew, becoming bigger by the day. Nights I'd hear it growing, straining toward the moon, a sound like an old man getting out of bed. Soon the mulberry was as tall as our house, and there wasn't enough sweat in my father's body to even muster a decent speech about taking it down anymore. So my father stopped speaking of the mulberry, and the mulberry became my tree.

My tree, it turned out, was a sanctuary, a place where my father's wishes and waves did not push against me, could not even touch me. This, too, I learned by accident. One day, the neighbor's cat, Mrs. Whiskers, a loaf of lithe muscle and white fur, climbed into the mulberry, climbed higher and higher, moving from one branch to the next, sure as a monkey, until a strong wind rose up and grabbed every branch and every leaf of the mulberry and shook them hard, shook them like the wind was trying to shake a secret out of my tree. Mrs. Whiskers froze. Two minutes, three minutes, four, Mrs. Whiskers did not move, not even a twitch of her tail. So I started to climb, not because I cared about Mrs. Whiskers' well-being but because I saw a chance to be a hero, and I had always wondered what it felt like to be a hero. I still wonder.

But as I climbed, getting closer and closer to Mrs. Whiskers, still frozen, more stone than cat, a strange thing happened. I became light, so light that climbing felt like floating. Climbing higher in the mulberry, I did not feel my father's waves pushing against me. I climbed right past Mrs. Whiskers to the highest stout branch of the mulberry, and there I stood, like a sailor in the rigging, as light and alive as the leaves that shimmied and chattered all around me.

To unite with my father, I had to leave my father. This I knew instinctually, this truth an innate part of me. From Jesus to James Dean, this is how fathers and sons have always found each other.

The very next day I started my preparations in secret. The plywood and two-by-fours I stole from a neighbor's garage. The hammer I took from my father's workbench, which was only a workbench in theory, never having been used for any work. The nails I pulled from the fences I passed walking to and from school. I spent hours pounding those nails straight with my father's hammer. I sang "John Henry" while I worked.

The construction took weeks, but I didn't mind. I savored the process: moving through the canopy, branch to branch, like a squirrel, quick and sure; analyzing area and angles, math suddenly concrete and important. The heft of lumber, the crack of hammer against nail, time and sweat, my time and sweat, creating, I reveled in it all. And when it was all done, I had my spot. Not so much a treehouse, but a solid platform. Big enough to hold two buckets for catching rainwater while also leaving room for me to sleep. Perfect.

I told my father at breakfast. His waves always diminished during meals, a kind of low tide that could be brought on by a bowl of Rice Krispies or a ribeye or a chocolate ice cream cone. It didn't matter. My father's waves weakened no matter what he was eating. That morning he was eating cinnamon toast. I can still smell it, like buttery cotton candy. And I can still taste the fear I had in me, bile burning at the back of my throat as I opened my mouth to speak: "I'll be moving out this afternoon." I waited, unsure what to expect.

My father raised his head, chewing his cinnamon toast gentle as a heifer. He raised one eyebrow, too. I braced for more, but it never came. There was just that eyebrow, curved like a wave, ushering/ shunting me toward my tree. As I left the house, I listened to my father sucking cinnamon sugar from his fingertips.

My first few days in the tree, I couldn't sit still. I moved among the branches, luxuriating in having to carry only my own weight. Just my own breath, just my own bones. Moving felt so good that I couldn't sleep. I spent nights teaching myself to dance. In a fork near the top of the canopy, I did the rhumba. Closer to my platform, I grasped the thick center of the tree and swung myself around it, sometimes quick, a flashy jitterbug move, sometimes slow, a stiff waltz. On my platform I worked on my breakdancing, spinning on my back until the stars became streaks of white light etched across the night sky. And each night my mulberry grew, groaning like that old man getting out of bed, inching me closer to the starlight.

During daylight I moved more slowly, conserving my energy. I would hop from branch to branch like a sparrow, eating mulberries as I went, imagining that I had eaten so many that their juice stained my tongue a permanent dark purple. And as I ate and hopped about I spoke to my tree, always speaking the same two sentences, "What's next, Tree? What's next?" Those two sentences became my birdsong, blending with the warble of the doves, the chirps of the starlings, the shrieks of the blue jays, music that I captured with my ears and stored in my heart and danced to each night.

But I didn't talk to my tree to make music. I talked to my tree to find answers. To unite with my father I first had to leave my father. This truth lived in my bones. The leaving I had figured out on my own, but now I needed help. "What's next, Tree? What's next?"

One rainy day, my answer finally blossomed in my tree's voice. That rain had been especially harsh and heavy. Bullet-sized drops ripped through the canopy of leaves overhead and clattered against my platform like marbles rolling down a stairwell. The sound of that rain obliterated my questions and swallowed my birdsong. That rain soaked my clothes and pounded my flesh until my legs and arms tingled. And finally, that rain made me think about my father. I tried to imagine what he was doing at that very moment. I tried to imagine him standing by our kitchen window watching the rain hammer the earth and flow through streets and yards. I tried to imagine his voice, too, was swallowed by the storm, but still he spoke. I tried to imagine the movement of his lips reflected in the window. I tried to imagine those lips mouthing the words *come home* over and over again, his lips puckering into a soft kiss with every *home*. And at that moment I felt heavy, heavier than I had ever felt in my tree.

Then, the inevitable. The rain stopped. The sun punched through the retreating clouds and the world filled with a hazy golden light. Steam rose off every surface. And then, the miraculous. "Just dance." My tree spoke with a voice like a gospel song, deep and smooth.

"What's next, Tree? What's next?" I had to be sure.

The steam rising off my platform undulated like a church lady feeling the spirit. "Just dance," said my tree's gospel-song voice.

I redoubled my dancing efforts. In addition to my regular nighttime dance routines, I began dancing during the day as well. I no longer hopped from branch to branch gobbling berries. I now danced from branch to branch gobbling berries. I'd Cabbage Patch the length of long thin branches, then do The Pony back the other way. I embraced thicker vertical limbs in a Tango, the mulberry bark rough against my cheek. I twerked and twisted, did The Robot and The Running Man, spent hours trying to teach squirrels The Electric Slide, all while the sun streaming through the leaves draped my every movement in an aura of pale-green light. When I needed to rest, I'd get down on my belly and do The Worm until I collapsed into sleep. I didn't speak anymore during the days because I didn't have to. I had my answer. But still, every once in a while, I'd hear my tree whisper: "Just dance." And those words would enter me and transform into helium, and I'd feel myself getting lighter and lighter.

As my days changed, so did my nights. Nights I stuck to my platform. Nights I stuck to spinning on my back. And I got good at spinning, going faster and faster each night until I sometimes felt I was more top than boy. And always there was the starlight overhead, spun into shiny pinstripes, cutting across the night sky. And as I spun and marveled at the starlight, I'd listen to my tree groaning like an old man getting out of bed, my tree ever stretching toward the moon, bringing me closer and closer to the starlight.

Yet some nights as I spun, I'd feel my tree changing underneath me and see the starlight changing too, getter brighter, thicker, and I'd feel doubts creeping up on me. A new question filled my mouth, which I'd let leak out into the dark: "When, Tree? When?"

"When, Tree? When?" I asked that question 1001 times, and then I never asked it again. Here's why.

One night the air was thick with heat. Sweat pooled on my platform as I spun. By this time my tree had grown so tall that I thought I might be able to touch the streaks of starlight. As I spun I raised my arms, arched my back a bit more, stretched, grasped at starlight just out of my reach. My tree grew and groaned, but that night my tree's groaning did not sound like an old man getting out of bed. Now my mulberry groaned like an old man praying for death. For the first time, I worried about my tree. Again, the question spilled out of me as I spun, "When, Tree? When?" over and over again, "When, Tree? When?" Perhaps I hoped this mantra could comfort us both. I stretched and reached for the starlight.

Yet my questions seemed to have no impact. The mulberry's groans grew louder and louder, grew more desperate. I could feel their thunder in my chest. I started to weep. But still I spun and grasped at the air awash in the groans of my tree.

"When, Tree? When?"

Starlight inches from my grasp, groans like prayers for death vibrating my ribs.

"When, Tree? When?"

Starlight centimeters from my grasp, groans like prayers for death rattling my ribs.

"When, Tree? When?"

Starlight millimeters from my grasp, groans like prayers for death cracking my ribs.

"When, Tree? When?"

Starlight a frog's hair from my grasp, groans like prayers for death pulverizing my ribs, and just then I heard a voice like a gospel song.

"Now."

Once more I grasped out, and I felt streaks of starlight fill each hand. A warmth entered me. I felt it in my lungs, hot and alive, mixing with my breath. Felt it zipping up and down my arms and legs, traveling through my bones. And then I felt it in my chest, stitching back and forth, back and forth where once my ribs had been, stitching back and forth, back and forth until a cage of starlight surrounded my heart.

I felt my back leaving the platform first, then mulberry leaves brushing past my face, my limbs. Then I was part of the night sky. I hovered, supported by thousands of threads of starlight. The air around me tasted sweet as bubblegum, the earth below just the twinkle of distant porch lights. All the starlight began to undulate, rising and falling, pushing forward, rising and falling, pushing me forward. I rode that starlight. I trusted that starlight. It propelled me across the sky like a meteor and finally dropped me at my father's back door.

I knocked once, then turned the knob. The door opened. Standing in the doorway, I saw my father's back as he leaned over the kitchen sink filling a glass with water.

"I'm home," I said.

My father did not turn to look at me.

He snapped off the faucet, raised one heel off the ground, and moonwalked, whoosh, whoosh, whoosh backward across the linoleum floor to me. And when he reached me, he grabbed my hand with his free palm and we both spun around, turning our backs to the kitchen. Looking out the open door I could see my mulberry, and I could see the starlight. My father handed me his glass. I lifted it to my lips. Cool water flooded my mouth, my throat. And together we moonwalked, whoosh, whoosh, whooshing back into our home, together.

R.J. Becomes a Piston

*The greatest recorded number of
consecutive sit-ups on a hard surface
without feet pinned or knees bent is
25,222 in 11 hours and 14 minutes by
R____ J____ K_____, age 8, at the
Idaho Falls High School Gymnasium on
December 23, 1972.*
--Guinness Book of
World Records 1978

Before he becomes a piston, R.J. is a heavy bag.

"Hey, Spaz."

"Nice glasses, Spaz."

"Why do you walk like a girl, Spaz?"

"Heard you're going to get jumped today, Spaz."

The blows come all day long. Each one lands with a pop, a sting like a gloved fist striking flesh. Each one sends shockwaves rippling through R.J.

Before he becomes a piston, R.J. is a carnival barker's megaphone.

The thought never forms in R.J.'s head, just comes booming out of his mouth when the gym teacher threatens sit-ups for the whole class: "I'm not scared of sit-ups. I can do more sit-ups than you." The voice doesn't feel like his own. It rattles R.J.'s back teeth as he speaks. Two sentences born as a bluff grasping toward hope.

Before he becomes a piston, R.J. is a Rorschach test.

Look at him laying straight and stiff on the slick gym floor. What do you see? Is it a dead man? Is it Sleeping Beauty?

See how he's interlaced his fingers behind his head, bending his arms into triangles? Do you see a boy with wings? Do you see a boy restrained?

Before he becomes a piston, R.J. is a spring.

Sit-up, sit-up, sit-up. Just an elongated nod, really. Raise the head, curl the neck, and keep going. A little grunt to get started and then a wave of momentum, a release of tension, a changing of form. Coil and stretch, coil and stretch. Natural as a heartbeat.

Before he becomes a piston, R.J. is a nursery-school music box.

I'm a little teapot, short and stout. Here is my handle. Here is my spout. When I get all steamed up hear me shout. Tip me over and pour me out. The song, bouncy and silly and stupid and fun, fills R.J.'s whole head. It drowns out the voices of the children swirling around him, suffocates the ghosts of those voices, too.

Up. Down. Up. Down. Up. Hear. Me. Shout. Nursery song becomes work song. R.J. moves in time with the lyrics.

R.J. becomes a piston. It happens in the middle of his five hundredth sit-up. Clarity arrives like a thunderclap.

Thousands and thousands and thousands of parts. The Happiness Machine has more parts than there are birds in the sky. But RJ is the most important part, the one part driving the whole beautiful business. R.J. is the piston. Up. Down. Up. Down. Pumping away. R.J. makes the Happiness Machine go.

And R.J. is the biggest part. All the other Happiness Machine parts are tiny, nearly microscopic, weightless. They float through the air, inconspicuous as dust motes and dandruff, but when RJ starts pumping, when R.J. keeps himself going, all those tiny, tiny parts spring to life, spinning and turning and whirring together, precise as watch works.

The spinning parts of the Happiness Machine pull in all the darkness around them, even the dark thoughts swirling in R.J.'s head, even the ghosts of those dark thoughts. The Happiness Machine grabs it all and grinds it down to something finer than ash, and the Happiness Machine blows those fine dark remains sky high, blows them out above the clouds, out into the cold, silent corners of outer space.

Sit-up, sit-up, sit-up. R.J. feels the light revealed by the Happiness Machine rippling around him, feels it moving through him like electricity. The air around him smells bakery sweet. Sit-up, sit-up, sit-up. He parts his teeth and opens wide, tastes that sweetness coating his tongue like cotton candy melting in a greedy mouth. But he has to keep going. Sit-up, sit-up, sit-up. From bluff to hope, he keeps going.

Mrs. Cinnamon

Jimmy plucks two yellow leaves shaped like fists. He passes them around for inspection, to Bumpo, to No No, the kids who never leave Jimmy's side, the moons that orbit planet Jimmy Dawson. He snatches the leaves back, tears them up, rolls them into a scrap of notebook paper, seals his creation with his spit, a kiss along the seam, strikes the lighter he filched from the gas station, and smokes.

Pocket lint, a pigeon feather, Kool Aid powder, a puff of brown dog hair light and airy as spun sugar, most often, stray bits of vegetation. Jimmy Dawson will roll anything handy into a scrap of notebook paper and smoke it while hanging out in Dead Man's Woods, the narrow strip of maple trees and undergrowth and trash that borders the playground of St. Luke's Catholic School. Once, not so long ago, the story went, a body had been found in Dead Man's Woods.

Standing among the shadows of Dead Man's Woods, the smell of damp earth everywhere, they pass the notebook cigarette around, an orange flame racing up it, devouring it. Everybody takes a hit or two, Jimmy, Bumpo, No No, and electricity crackles along Jimmy's every nerve. They all say this is the stuff, so much better than last time, this stuff is getting us high, we're flying now, man, we need to remember where we found this stuff, their words ritualistic, like prayer. The end-of-recess bell chiming in the distance sounds like a cheering crowd to Jimmy, recognition for the amazing Jimmy Dawson, defiant and free and only in the second grade.

A loud rustling of leaves and suddenly Cody Lawson stands before Jimmy and the boys. Cody's red hair looks like a setting sun.

"Dudes, you better come on. Mrs. Snapp looks pissed."

"Get out of here, Queer Boy," Jimmy says.

"Ha. Queer Boy," Bumpo says, and his lumpy belly starts to shake.

"Yeah. Queer Boy," No No adds, as if to make it unanimous.

More than he wants his parents to get back together, more than he wants to be a professional wrestler when he grows up and to fly around the ring in a shiny mask and call himself Rey Mysterio III, Cody Lawson wants to feel one of Jimmy Dawson's homemade cigarettes between his lips, smell the smoke as it settles into his clothes, his hair. And not because Cody wants to smoke or wants to get high, but because he longs to shine in the reflected glow of the Amazing Jimmy Dawson.

"Don't call me Queer Boy," Cody says.

"Why not?" Jimmy says.

"Cause I'm not queer."

"Yeah ya are. Running in here talking about 'Mrs. Snapp, Mrs. Snapp,' like you're scared of that bitch."

"I'm not scared."

"Or maybe you love her. Oh, Mrs. Snapp, Mrs. Snapp."

"Mrs. Snapp, Mrs. Snapp," Bumpo and No No sing with high girly voices. They make kissing sounds, their faces pinched like closed fists.

"I hate Mrs. Snapp," Cody says.

Jimmy leans in so close that Cody can smell the burnt leaves and ashy notebook paper on his breath. "Prove it," Jimmy says.

"Mrs. Snapp is a bitch, bitchbitch," Cody hisses, like a person trying to get a friend's attention in church. The words feel slick on his tongue. They taste like iron.

No No and Bumpo fall to the ground laughing. "That don't prove nothing," Jimmy says.

"So what am I supposed to do?"

"Kill Mrs. Cinnamon," Jimmy says, "that will prove it."

No No jumps to his feet. "Yeah, yeah, yeah," he says. "She loves that stupid guinea pig." His thin arms flap with excitement.

"I hate that thing," Bumpo says, red-faced from the strain of raising his bulky frame. "It stinks. Smells like cabbage."

"Why would I kill Mrs. Cinnamon?" Cody says.

"To prove you're not queer. You kill Mrs. Cinnamon, and we won't call you Queer Boy anymore," Jimmy says.

"But how am I supposed to kill a guinea pig."

"Be out here tomorrow at recess. I'll bring the pig, and you can kill it."

"How are you going to get Mrs. Cinnamon?" Cody asks.

"I'll get her," Jimmy says, "Just be here."

Jimmy's eyes look black and hollow, like the barrels of a pair of pistols.

"Okay," Cody says.

The end-of-recess bell stopped ringing a long time ago.

*

Jimmy Dawson, Bumpo, and No No are waiting for Cody when he walks into Dead Man's Woods.

"Queer Boy's here," Jimmy says.

Bumpo reaches into the front pouch of his gray hoodie and Mrs. Cinnamon appears in his hand like a half-hearted magic trick. He passes her to Cody.

Cody holds Mrs. Cinnamon in his right arm, cradles her against his hip. Her short brown fur looks shiny, almost varnished. She blinks as if she's trying to make sense of her new surroundings. She feels warm and surprisingly heavy to Cody, like a loaf of his mother's homemade bread.

"How'd you get her?" Cody asks.

"Easy. Bitch is stupid. So do it, Queer Boy," Jimmy says.

"Yeah, yeah," No No says. He starts to jump around. His whip-thin arms and legs churn the air. He is a dancing skeleton from a Halloween cartoon. Bumpo just tilts his head and looks at Cody. Jimmy Dawson stares at Cody, his eyes a pair of pistol barrels. Cody feels Mrs. Cinnamon's heartbeat, quick, against his fingertips.

Cody wants to say, "How am I supposed to kill her?" But he knows that would sound queer, so instead he says, "Can we smoke first?"

"He wants to smoke, he wants to smoke," No No says, launching into a more-frantic bouncing.

"Sure," Jimmy says. "Grab something."

"Something?" Cody says.

"Grab some leaves, Queer Boy, some leaves," Jimmy says.

"Leaves, leaves, Queer Boy," No No adds, a hyperactive echo. Bumpo just shakes his head like he's watching a shortstop boot an easy groundball.

Cody looks for leaves. They're everywhere in Dead Man's Woods. On the ground, dead and brown and crunchy, bigger than his hand, or small and green on shoots that dot the damp soil. On the bushes, just starting to turn, some still green, some yellowing like old age, a few dotted with ominous black growths. Leaves high in the canopies above him make a sound like chattering teeth when the wind blows. But Cody just grabs the first thing within reach of his free left hand, because he wants to look sure of himself, because he doesn't want to give anybody another opportunity to call him Queer Boy. He puts a few dark green leaves, shorter than his thumb and shaped like footballs, into Jimmy Dawson's outstretched hand. The flesh of Jimmy's palm feels cold and moist.

"Good choice, Queer Boy," Jimmy says. He pulls on old spelling test from his back pocket, rips off the top corner, rolls the leaves into the paper, and kisses it closed. He pulls out the lighter, and they smoke.

They have to pass around the lighter with the cigarette because it won't stay lit, but they all take turns, the hiss and click of the lighter, the sucking sound of deep inhalation. And Jimmy and Bumpo and No No all say that this is good stuff, that they are really getting high now, and then Bumpo holds the lighter for Cody, so Cody can smoke with his left hand, while Mrs. Cinnamon squirms against him in his right hand, and after he smokes Cody says, "Shit yeah, man," and a taste like fireworks lingers on his tongue long after he has passed the cigarette on to No No.

But then the cigarette is gone, and two words bloom in its wake and fill all of Dead Man's Woods.

"Do it," Jimmy Dawson says.

And Cody feels a tornado spinning in his head, and he feels every-thing inside of him shrinking, his heart and lungs and stomach shrivel-ing until they are as tiny and wrinkled as raisins and he is nearly hollow, and he wants to find a way to stop time, but he can't, and Bumpo, with his head tilted, is still looking at Cody, and No No is still bouncing, he might even be hovering in the air, like a hummingbird, and Jimmy Dawson is staring at Cody with his pistol-barrel eyes.

Cody lifts Mrs. Cinnamon, holds her out in front of him, using both hands to grip her just below her front legs. He looks as if he might be trying to estimate her weight. She wiggles in Cody's hands. Her rear end swings back and forth, a kind of furry pendulum. In the distance a blue jay squawks, "Thief, thief."

"Do it, Queer Boy," Jimmy Dawson says, his voice sharp as a police whistle.

And Cody thinks, *God, help me, tell me what to do.*

And there is silence.

Then the squawk of the jay, "Thief, thief."

More silence.

Cody looks at Mrs. Cinnamon dangling in the air before him. She stops squirming. Her dark eyes become watery. She speaks to Cody.

Her voice is warm, but serious, sounds just like the voice of the woman who reads the news on the country radio station that Cody's mom always listens to.

Mrs. Cinnamon says, "Do it, Cody. It's okay. I want you to. I must die, so you can be saved. It's like Jesus."

And Cody feels his legs wobbling underneath him. He knows what he must do, but Cody Lawson can't do it.

Dead Man's Woods fades away, replaced by a huge arena, spotlights illuminating a blue-grey wrestling ring. Bumpo and No No and Jimmy Dawson are replaced by a cheering crowd of thousands. Cody's mom and dad sit next to each other in the front row, hands mingling in a bucket of popcorn. Gone is Cody Lawson. In his place stands Rey Mys-terio III. He wears shiny gold tights and red wrestling boots; a gold and red mask hides his face. And he is locked in combat with a black-hearted opponent who wears a fur-covered mask and calls himself the Wild Boar. And Rey Mysterio III knows that the Wild Boar is so determinedly evil that the only way to stop him is to choke him out. And Rey III has got ahold of the Wild Boar with his left hand, and he sees his opening, so he goes for it because he knows when he beats the Wild Boar the whole world will know how tough he is. Everyone in the arena will rise and cheer. His parents will cling to each other, the way they used to, as they jump and scream, "Rey. Rey. Rey." And from that moment onward, people's eyes will grow big and their mouths will drop open when he walks by. When they speak to him, they will call him Champ. They will do what he tells them to do. They will fear him. They will love him.

Quick as a lightning bolt, Rey Mysterio III has his right hand around the Wild Boar's throat and he is squeezing, taking the fight, the air, out of the Wild Boar. Rey Mysterio III feels the electricity of impending victory dancing along his spine, the roaring of the crowd now deafening.

A slap against the ear, a ringing like church bells, knuckles against nose, a warm trickle of blood. Something has gone terribly wrong. The Wild Boar's cronies must have run into the ring. Rey Mysterio III is down. A boot to the gut. A boot to the gut.

When Cody manages to roll onto his back Bumpo pounces on him, uses his knees to pin Cody's shoulders to the ground. And floating above Bumpo's meaty face is Jimmy Dawson's head, and Jimmy says, "You crazy fuck."

And Cody can't see No No, but he can hear him saying, "Ohshitohshitohshit." And Cody can hear Mrs. Cinnamon racing through the underbrush, gone. And Cody can hear Mrs. Cinnamon singing a celebration song as she runs. She sings, "Back from the dead and free as a spirit. It's like Jesus."

Cody feels the damp of Dead Man's Woods seeping into his clothes as Mrs. Cinnamon's song grows faint.

Sousathon

There are the band kids. And there are the Leys.

The band kids are all weird proportions. They are too-short legs and too-big bellies. They are heads large as bowling balls or tiny as fists. As they move into formation on the high school parking lot, the asphalt still cool in the gray light of dawn, the band kids look as if they were once seventy-five perfect teenage bodies that somehow got blown apart and haphazardly reassembled, like the second tuba's arms might actually belong to the red-headed drummer, and the red-headed drummer's big feet might belong to the first trombone.

The band kids are thick polyester uniforms that are too hot in the summer and too cold in the winter and always smell like a damp basement. The band kids are dingy brass buttons and epaulets molting gold fringe. The band kids are church-camp shenanigans. They are sterling math grades. They are comic books and sci-fi novels and the same Monty Python lines repeated over and over and over again.

And the band kids are cheap, common. You can't swing a dead cat in the halls of Wendell Willkie High School without hitting a band kid. But the Leys, they are precious because they are rare. Ashley, Bailey, Caley, Kaley, and Miley. That's it. That's all there are.

The Leys are diamonds. They shine. Hair like spun sunlight cascading down past their shoulders, smiles like fireworks, blue eyes dancing like the northern lights, and each Ley grasps in her right hand a shiny silver baton that twirls and twirls and twirls at ten thousand rpms, humming through the cool morning air. Those batons never stop twirling, never stop shining.

Nobody twirls like the Leys. Nobody. Nobody's baton spins faster. Nobody's baton flies higher. Nobody's baton responds to each muscle twitch, to each flash of thought the way a Ley baton does. In the hands of a Ley, a baton is not even a baton. In the hands of a Ley, a baton becomes spinning silver light locked in a dance led by the Ley.

Each Ley dancing with her silver light. Each Ley dancing with the four other Leys dancing with their silver lights. Every move synchronized. Every move perfect. It's a hell of a show that's brought the crowd to the high school parking lot at the crack of dawn.

And the band? Well, it's hard to dance without music. Some of the band kids will fool themselves into thinking they are shining. But the band kids are the moon, any shine that they muster just a muted reflection of the light of the Leys.

*

The grandpas have come in their seed-company ballcaps, the grandmas in too-big hoodies. Wild-eyed toddlers weave through the crowd pursued by tired mothers. The high school kids spread out throughout the parking lot, sorted into cliques, neat and precise. Here a huddle of stoners, there a knot of preps. The theater kids over there, and the mathletes over there, and there are the Jesus kids, and there are the jocks, and all of the high school kids are trying to play it cool, and all of the high school kids are wondering what it would be like to get close to a Ley.

As Caley is twirling for all of them, as she weaves a turn of her wrist, a twitch of a finger, into spinning silver light, she feels it, heavy in her chest, the secret she always carries, a cinderblock locked in her heart. Sometimes the weight of the secret makes it hard for Caley to breathe. Some days she swears she can feel the cinderblock growing bigger, heavier. Today she fears the secret is growing so big and so heavy that it will crack her open like an egg, and that secret will come tumbling out of her for everybody to see.

And then everybody will know that Caley doesn't want to be a Ley anymore.

*

The band kids didn't invite the Leys. The band kids had wanted to play John Philip Sousa songs for twenty-four straight hours. Just music. That's what the band kids wanted.

"We can charge people."

"They'll love it!"

"A fundraiser."

"A bandathon."

"A Sousathon!"

"Sou Sa Thon, Sou Sa Thon." The chant passed from one band kid to another. It rattled the risers in the band room.

The band director had to raise his baton to restore order. "Yes, this is a fantastic idea. And the Leys can twirl while you play."

A groan filled the band room. "Why?" the band kids demanded. "Why do we need the Leys?"

The band director ignored their questions because sometimes the truth is too much. He couldn't bring himself to look into all those sad, mismatched faces and explain that Sousa was music, just music, and the band kids, they also were music, just music, but the Leys, the Leys were diamonds, and only diamonds draw top dollar.

*

Caley's problem with being a Ley is simple. It's all the other Leys.

Caley's problem with all the other Leys is complex.

*

For the first two hours of the Sousathon, Caley is a raw nerve. She's right in the middle of the twirling, dancing Leys, Ashley and Bailey to her right, Kaley and Miley to her left. Perfect hair and perfect smiles and perfect spinning silver light to her right. Perfect hair and perfect smiles and perfect spinning silver light to her left. This is the burden of being a Ley: unflinching perfection. *What if my hair doesn't have the bounce it should? What if my smile droops? What if*—and this is the thought really grating on Caley, the thought jangling every part of her like an electric current—*what if I drop the baton?*

The problem with perfection is there's no wiggle room.

Caley is supposed to keep her eyes straight ahead, study the horizon or pick out a face in the crowd and focus on just that face. It's so hard to do. She wants to peek at the other Leys. Just a glance, a shifting of her eyes to the left, to the right, quick as hiccup, a second to compare, to see that she is keeping up, a flash of reassurance.

Or, just maybe, with a glance she could catch one of the other Leys. Maybe Ashley wouldn't be lifting her knees high enough or maybe Miley wouldn't be twirling fast enough. But what most nags at Caley, what makes it so hard to not look at the other Leys, is the thought that one of the other Leys might finally drop a baton. Like the moon landing, a Ley dropping a baton is an event that demands witness. The moment one of those spinning silver lights comes crashing down, worldviews change. The sound of a Ley-dropped baton clattering against the asphalt parking lot could set Caley free, could crumble the cinderblock in her heart.

Caley's never desired a sound so much in her life. She aches for it.

*

The band director designed the Sousathon flyers: SOUSATHON Featuring the AMAZING TWIRLING LEYS in graffiti letters surrounded by five batons across the top third of the page. Underneath, in smaller, rigid block letters: 24 Straight Hours of John Philip Sousa Marches and TWIRLING, TWIRLING, TWIRLING. A Feast for the Eyes and Ears. Food and Craft Booths. Bounce House. Fun for the Whole Family. $3.00 Per Person. All Proceeds Benefit the Wendell Willkie Marching Panthers.

*

It starts in Caley's right hand, her twirling hand. She feels it for the first time just as the voice of Mr. Gainer, history teacher and announcer for Wendell Willkie football, booms over the sound system: "Three hours. Three hours complete."

What Caley feels is an absence. Her hand is still there, and her baton is still there, but the boundary between the two has disappeared. It feels as if the baton is part of Caley. It feels as if Caley is part of the baton, part of that spinning silver light.

Caley's hand/Caley's spinning silver light weighs almost nothing. It's dandelion fluff on butterfly wings, and its spinning, its flying is no longer something Caley controls. It just happens, involuntary, like blinking, easy, like breathing.

Caley feels a lightening in her chest.

*

The band kids' parents distributed the Sousathon flyers. Took them to their workplaces, their friends' businesses. The dry cleaner, the honest mechanic on the east side of town, both drugstores, the gas stations, the florist, Jackson's Diner, the grocery store, the bar with good wings, the bar with shitty pool tables, the bank with the pretty tellers, they all posted the flyers. The band kids' parents pinned the flyers to church bulletin boards, stapled them to telephone poles, shoved them under the windshield wipers of strangers' cars in the Wal-Mart parking lot.

The band kids could not get away from those damn flyers, and every time they passed one, they felt it, a surge of pride, quickly beaten down by the five batons twirling across the top of the flyers.

*

For Sousathon, the band kids are not one big band; they are three smaller bands. For the Sousathon they are A, B, and C. A plays three songs, then B plays three songs, then C plays three songs. Repeat, repeat, repeat for twenty-four hours.

It's a matter of frailty, the band director says. It's about lips and lungs and tongues and how none of it is built to play marches for twenty-four straight hours. It's about insurance and liability and I've-got-a-mortgage-to-pay-and-can't-afford-to-lose-my-job-because-some-kid-got-hurt, the band director says.

The band kids refuse to let Sousathon feel like a sham. Sure, nobody is really playing for twenty-four straight hours, but the music never stops. The music is the thing. Horns will ring and flutes will sing and woodwinds will bleat and drums will beat for twenty-four hours nonstop, and that is the doing of the band kids. They are creating something this town has never seen before. And, damn, son, playing for eight hours in a day is no joke. How many other band kids have ever done that? I'll tell you how many. None. That's how many. You go, group A. You go, B. You go, C. Band kids out here making history. The band kids all agree.

A few of the band kids wonder aloud why the Leys have not also been broken into three groups. This question is their gift to the rest of the band kids. They pass it around, take turns mumbling, "Man, that Ley stuff must be so easy."

The band kids watch the always-dancing Leys with their spinning silver lights and wonder what it would be like to get close to a Ley.

*

It must be the movement. Maybe the constant spinning, spinning, spinning, spinning fuels a kind of hypnosis. Or maybe it's simpler than that. Maybe it's just an oversized version of the loosening of thought brought on by fatigue, but eight hours into the Sousathon, Caley has mostly lost track of where she ends and where the rest of the universe begins.

Caley sort of remembers where her arms and legs are, but she couldn't draw an accurate picture of them, couldn't give you directions to find them. Her limbs have become shape-shifting tricksters.

Each limb could be microscopic, just another atom, part of the air the town breathes. Her legs may be in some band kid's lungs right now. Her arms might be flying out of the bell of a trombone.

Each limb could be huge, sprawling like an American boomtown, an arm like Houston, a leg like LA, all pushing ever outward, overtaking fields and forests and mountain ranges, borders moving so fast the mapmakers can't keep up.

Caley's arms and legs are almost nowhere, so Caley's arms and legs are almost everywhere. It's a paradox that Caley can't put into words, but she knows it's true because she feels it in her heart. That paradox is a stiff ocean breeze whipping against the cinderblock hidden there, slow erosion, a lightening.

*

B is the worst band. B is squeaking clarinets and lost drummers and a lone tuba player whose lungs lack the oomph to generate a decent oompah. B takes Sousa marches and turns them into hikes through quicksand, plodding, fear-filled, hopeless slogs. Struggling only makes things worse. And it keeps happening. There's a wave of relief for the B band kids every time they squawk the final note of their third song, a moment to enjoy a deep breath and the polite applause of the crowd. But galloping in on the heels of that applause it comes, trepidation, panic. The B kids know, just six songs, and then they'll be back in the swamp.

The problem isn't just that B band is terrible. The problem is B band knows they are terrible. At the start of Sousathon, after they played, B would huddle, share advice and pep talk clichés.

"Try wetting the reed more."

"Watch me. I'll let you know when to come in."

"We got this now."

"We're gonna kill it."

But now, thirteen hours into Sousathon, when not playing, B band kids just stand around wearing the wide-eyed, open mouthed expressions of the shell shocked, the only words of encouragement coming from the weak-winded tuba player: "It's more than half over."

The crowd doesn't recognize B's pain. Crisp, bouncing Sousa, awkward slogging Sousa. For the crowd, it's all the same Sousa. It's all white noise playing behind the Leys' twirling.

But Caley's stomach churns for B band. She feels the joy seeping out of them, feels their embarrassment and despair. She feels it because she is part of the band, and they are part of her. Thirteen hours into Sousathon and Caley's body no longer holds Caley at all. Thirteen hours into Sousathon, and Caley is everywhere and part of almost everything.

*

Caley got a *C-* on her transcendentalism test in sophomore American lit. She hadn't had time to find the SparkNotes for any of the readings. She tried to find a *Walden* movie, but only turned up a meandering documentary that put her to sleep. As she took the test, the only thing she remembered from her textbook was a line drawing in the Emerson section.

The drawing was mostly legs, long, thin, spidery legs dwarfing the hills that shared the foreground. Atop the legs sat one large, veiny eyeball. Something in its big black pupil spoke of longing to Caley. The giant eyeball wore a hat, a sort of a fedora, but built for a giant eyeball.

The essay question on the test asked about the Over-soul. Caley guessed the giant eyeball must be the Over-soul. On her test she wrote how she felt sorry for the Over-soul, forced to march barefoot through a desolate landscape, unable to even blink, a rumpled hat its only shelter. Caley's teacher filled the margins around Caley's essay with bright red question marks and frowny faces.

Fifteen hours into Sousathon and Caley is rethinking her feelings about the Over-soul, rethinking what the world might feel like to a giant eyeball out for a hike.

Fifteen hours into Sousathon and Caley is rethinking her relationship to the world, trying to grasp how she is almost everywhere at once, and the world feels as if it's moving through her.

*

Caley likes the name Over-soul. In the eighteenth hour of Sousathon she mouths *Over-soul* as she smiles and her baton twirls, silver light spinning, spinning, spinning. She mouths *Over-soul* as the frustrations of the band kids and the restlessness of the crowd all become part of her, move through her like oxygen, like blood. But she doesn't feel like a giant walking eyeball wearing a hat, not really.

Caley feels more like she's become a giant eyeball floating through the world, windblown and free. A giant floating eyeball expanding, expanding. A giant floating eyeball of porous flesh laced with a dense network of nerves, wild knots and tangles of nerves running everywhere. And those nerves convert all the light rushing into the growing dark pupil into crystal-sharp images. And those nerves vibrate with and relay every sound swirling around the giant eyeball. And those nerves taste, taste the humidity in the air, taste the sweat and musk of every body passing through its porous flesh. And those nerves feel, share in the physical sensations of every living entity the giant floating eyeball encompasses. The thirst of an oak tree two blocks away, the tingling in the lips of the C band trumpet player starting on her third song, the pain in Miley's left knee, the crick in Bailey's neck, the giant floating eyeball feels it all.

But mostly what the eyeball feels is secrets. The nerves of the eyeball creep like kudzu, wiggle their way into even the most staunchly locked hearts. The nerves find, Caley finds, a secret like a pile of moldering leaves in the band director's heart. A grandma's heart holds a swinging sledgehammer. The band kids' hearts hold flocks of bats, a couple of rusting ship anchors, a bulldozer, an old rotary phone that rings and rings and rings, and more razor blades than Caley can count.

But it's the Leys' hearts that are most amazing. Ashley's heart holds a tire fire, Bailey's holds a train wreck. Kaley's heart is home to a rabid opossum, Miley's hides a hurricane. Caley takes them all in. All the Leys are part of Caley now. All the Leys' secrets are part of Caley. And as Caley continues to grow, she continues to disappear. She takes in everything and every secret around her, and her own secret starts to feel smaller and smaller. Her own secret, the cinderblock in her heart, might even be crushed under the weight of all the new secrets running in.

Caley's lost track of her baton. It's probably still spinning, spinning, spinning, silver light cutting through the midnight darkness hanging over the Wendell Willkie High School parking lot. Or maybe it's clattered to earth. Maybe it lays on the asphalt inert.

It really doesn't matter. Caley is still growing.

Judy's Pitch

Longest home run

*In a minor league game at
Emeryville Ball Park, CA on 4 Jul
1929, Roy Edward "Dizzy" Carlyle
(1900-56) hit a homerun measured
at 618 ft.*

--Guinness Book of World Records,
1994

The pitch felt good, the laces whispering against the tips of my fingers as the ball left my hand.

The pitch looked good. A 2-2 fastball, low and away, off the plate. A pitch Dizzy couldn't do anything with. A pitch Dizzy would fish for. Dizzy would always fish for that outside pitch.

The pitch felt and looked so good that, for the first and only time, I mouthed a spontaneous dedication, blessing that ball as it hummed toward home plate: For Judy, a pitch as powerful and sure as our love.

And Dizzy did fish, lunging for Judy's pitch with all the hope and fury of a blind man throwing a punch.

And Dizzy made thunder. Judy's pitch came off of Dizzy's bat with a crack that shook the earth. Every seat in Emeryville Ball Park vibrated in the wake of Dizzy's swing. I still feel that crack from Dizzy's bat. It still rattles through my ribs.

And Dizzy and I both just stood there, hands on our hips, and watched as that ball took off at five hundred miles an hour hell bent for the horizon. Before it even cleared the infield that ball started glowing red, throbbing like hot coals. Glowing and racing and rising, up, up, up.

And just before that ball cleared the outfield wall, still going up, up, up, it grew a comet's tail, a stream of yellow and orange fire dancing across California's cloudless blue sky. Even from the pitcher's mound, I felt the heat of that comet's tail. It marked me, burned me like a nuclear flash. I still wear that burn, my skin still raw and tight. And it hurts. Some days, when I brush up against the empty air surrounding me, brush up against those places where Judy should be but isn't, my whole body tingles, and I am still standing in the heat of that homerun.

When that ball cleared the park, it was three thousand feet high and still rising. The next day the newspaper said it finally came down in a drugstore parking lot, 618 feet from where it had first made contact with Dizzy's bat, the longest homerun in the history of baseball.

But the newspaper lied. That ball never came down. All these years later it's still out there, going up, up, up, rocketing through outer space now. I know because if I look hard into the night sky and pinch my eyes almost shut I can still see it, a red and orange and yellow streak passing across the silver face of the moon, the love that Judy and I shared hot and beautiful in some other universe.

Noah Filkins Is an Amazing Lover

Noah Filkins is an amazing lover. Noah Filkins is an amazing lover. Noah Filkins is an amazing lover. Noah Filkins is

I'm flat on my back, under my bed, writing on the bedframe when the nurse comes to get me. I hear the whoosh of my door opening, turn my head to see shoes coming toward me, running shoes, pink and light and airy as cotton candy. All the nurses wear them, running shoes in circus colors. Send in the clowns. I curse under my breath. A couple *shits* and a *Godamnit.* I thought I had more time.

I shuffle the black Sharpie into my pocket. The vapors of the ink drying on the bedframe make me lightheaded. The cold of the tile floor cuts through my tracksuit, sinks into my bones. I grope for a cover story. *I dropped something.* Or maybe, *Something seemed off with the bed. I was checking the bed, trying to fix it.* No. Better just say I dropped something, or I thought I dropped something. *I thought I dropped my book last night when I fell asleep reading. I thought maybe it was under the bed.*

The nurse has a voice like a kindergarten teacher, sing-songy and stern at the same time: "Mrs. Filkins, hellloooo, are you ready for your big day? Mrs. Filkins? Mrs. Filkins? Mrs. Filkins! Are you okay, Mrs. Filkins? Don't move. I'll get help. Everything is going to be okay, Mrs. Filkins."

I stick one hand out from under the bed and give the nurse a thumbs up. I say, "I'm fine," but the nurse keeps on jabbering like she doesn't hear me, like my words get lost in the mattress above me.

"You just relax and don't move and everything will be fine. We'll have you out of there and on your feet lickety-split." Panic sharpens the ends of each syllable.

I wiggle out from under my bed, reach for the side rails, pull myself upright. The nurse watches me the whole time, her face pretty and open and amazed. She looks like a kid watching a man eat fire. "Ta-dah."

"Why, Mrs. Filkins, I'm so glad to see you're alright. You really scared me. What in the world were you doing down there?"

"I thought I dropped a book." I wave my hand in the air near my face, swatting away her follow-up questions before they have a chance to form.

"Well, we should get going. You don't want to miss your own party. Everyone is in the dayroom waiting for you already. You're going to have a happy, happy 107. I just know it."

"Yes, happy, happy."

"Let's go join the fun."

"Yes. I just need a moment to freshen up."

Alone in the bathroom, I squat and manage to squeeze in a few more on the underside of the sink. *Noah Filkins is an amazing lover. Noah Filkins is an amazing lover.* It's still not enough. It feels like it may never be enough.

The nurse calls to me through the locked door: "Come on, Birthday Girl. I think I smell cake."

*

Noah Filkins is an amazing lover.

That sentence is promise.

Noah Filkins is an amazing lover.

That sentence is a penance.

Noah Filkins is an amazing lover.

That sentence is a part of me, like blood or breath, has been for over sixty years.

Noah Filkins is an amazing lover.

That sentence is the medicine to heal broken hearts.

Noah Filkins is an amazing lover.

That sentence is the weight that keeps me pinned to the earth.

*

I know it's a cliché, but it's also the truth. It wasn't planned. It just sort of happened. You know the story. You've heard it before.

Noah had been growing more distant. He spent more evenings puttering around alone in the garage, more nights falling asleep on the couch and never coming to bed. We'd been married close to thirty years. These things happen. There were never any angry words. There were just fewer words. Fewer stories and jokes. Fewer *thank you*s. For years Noah had been full of *thank you*s. We both had. Thank you for doing the dishes. Thank you for reminding me about my appointment. Thank you for calling the contactor. Thank you for listening, for helping, for caring, for loving me.

Of all the missing words, I missed the *thank you*s most of all, each one a small kindness, an intimacy.

And then there was Ben Knorr. For twenty odd years we had worked together at the elementary school. I taught second grade; Ben taught third, his classroom right next to mine. We ate lunch together, gossiped about the kids, their families, the other teachers. Ben's wife left him. Ben was heartbroken. Ben was full of *thank you*s. Thank you for listening. Thank you for caring. You see where this is going. You've heard this story before.

But it only happened the one time, just once. I swear. And afterward I felt hollow and ashamed. I never said anything, but somehow Noah found out, and it crushed him, broke him into ten thousand pieces.

How do you apologize for a mistake that shatters a person? How do you put them back together? For me, it starts and ends with the same sentence.

*

"Happy birthday," they all say in unison when the nurse walks me into the dayroom. I want to say they yell happy birthday or they cheer, but it's not like that. It's more like the perfunctory schoolroom Pledge of Allegiance. "OnenationunderGodindivisible." You know the drone. "Happy birthday." This time it's just one creaky voice. Just Frank. Poor Frank, always ten seconds behind the rest of the world.

They've shuffled the dayroom furniture, moved the tables and chairs into a kind of horseshoe, so walking into the dayroom feels like walking onto a stage to perform dinner theatre. I should be belting out show-tunes.

There's a cake, of course. It's the same big sheet cake we have for every celebration here. It's covered in white buttercream and ten flaming candles, and when the nurses cut into it, one side will be white cake and one side will be chocolate, and this will throw Dolores into a tizzy. What to do, what to do? Choices can be so hard. What if the white cake is the best? It's usually the best, right? But what if this time the chocolate is better? Dolores squints her eyes as she stares at the cake. Worry furrows her forehead. The debate has already started in her head. It's not really about cake. It's about opportunity costs, about missing out.

The singing starts when the nurse and I reach the center of the horseshoe. "Happy birthday to you, happy birthday to you," sing voices ragged with age and fatigue. I scan the faces. Nurses lean against the walls. They smile. They are all great smilers. It's part of their job, I think. They get paid to smile. They are professional smilers.

Residents fill the chairs. Many of them are like Frank and Dolores, confused, scared. Millie suffers from dementia and can never remember we have a nice cafeteria here. She spends hours every day agonizing about where her next meal will come from, hands clasped, praying for food. Every time a nurse rolls her into the cafeteria, Millie experiences a miracle. Hallelujah. Blessed be this lasagna. Blessed be this most holy lime Jell-O. This cake will be a miracle for Millie. Others are sharp as razors. Jinny paints beautiful watercolors of covered bridges and sagging barns. Bernie flirts with the nurses like a Vegas hustler.

Confused and scared or razor sharp, we're all old. We're all thin hair like corn silk and cardigan sweaters in July to stave off the chills. We're all joints that ache in the damp. We're all threadbare stories about our people departed. My Noah's been gone almost a decade. We never had children. My only sister died when I was just in my sixties. Every year a nurse will ask me, "Is there anybody you'd like to invite to your birthday party? Is there anybody we should call?"

"Call the cavalry," I say every year.

The singing builds to the big finish: ". . . birthday day to. . .." The nurses raise their hands to their chests, ready to clap, smiling the whole time. I want to pinch their cheeks. Some of the residents rock with excitement, happy for me, maybe, happy for the cake. I make a show of inhaling a big breath. My chest expands. My shoulders rise.

I lean down toward the cake, and then I blow. I get them all in my first try, all ten candles, every wavering flame, so much extinguished with a single big breath.

*

Two weeks after Noah found out about the affair, we were still rehashing the whole sorry thing, a kind of nightly call and response.

"Why?" Noah asked me, "Why?" This was the question he couldn't put down, the bone he couldn't stop chewing. The night my sentence was born, he didn't even look at me as he asked the question, just sat in his wingback chair studying the ceiling and listening to the Cubs game on the radio while I sat on the couch, a book of half-finished crossword puzzles in my lap.

"Why? What does he have that I don't?"

"It's not like that." The Cubs were down by six runs in the eighth. Noah's eyes never left the ceiling.

"Don't I protect you and take care of you? Don't I rub your shoulders when you tell me you've had a bad day at school? Don't I make sure all the bills are paid and the house isn't falling down? Don't I listen when you need to talk?"

"Noah, you're great. The best." The book of crossword puzzles thumped against the carpet as I rose from the couch to approach Noah. "You're all I want." I crouched down next his chair. The Cubs gave up a two-run homer, the hole suddenly deeper. I rested my hand on Noah's forearm.

"There has to be something."

"It just happened. I'm so sorry."

"Do I not satisfy you?" Noah's voice wavered and sputtered like a man struggling to pronounce a foreign phrase.

"Noah Filkins, you are an amazing lover." I rubbed Noah's forearm, my touch as light as breath. Goosebumps bloomed in the wake of my fingertips.

Noah turned to face me.

"It's true. I'll even put it in writing. Noah Filkins is an amazing lover." I tried to give Noah a silly smile, squinched up my eyes, curled my lips. "I'll write it a billion times."

And then it happened. The darkness that had lived in Noah's face for the past two weeks began to fracture. Something lighter started to show through the cracks.

"I'll start right now," I said. I walked over and picked the book of crossword puzzles off the carpet. I sat back down on the couch and found my pencil trapped between the cushions. I flipped to the first crossword puzzle, and in the white margin that ran across the top of the page I wrote: *Noah Filkins is an amazing lover.* Noah was still looking at me. I showed him the first page of the crossword puzzle book, showed him my sentence. I smiled at him and said, "One." I turned to the next page. "Only 999 million and change to go." I curved my back as I wrote, curled myself around that sentence, leaned into the work.

*

Noah Filkins is an amazing lover.

At first the sentence was easy, fun, a kind of game. I could get thirty-four *Noah Filkins is an amazing lover*s on a sheet of college-ruled notebook paper, one sentence on each line and two more in the white space at the top of the page. I'd rip the filled pages out of the notebook and leave them in places I knew only Noah would find them, on top of his workbench in the garage, in his underwear drawer, pressed between the pages of whatever book he happened to be reading, in the refrigerator taped to one of Noah's Budweisers. And I'd know when Noah found the sentences without him having to say a word. He'd come in from the garage with bounce in his step and give me a wink as he walked through the kitchen. He'd take a long, slow pull from a Budweiser and look at me over the top of the can, his eyebrows raised. And I would know, and he would know I knew.

I imagined each one of those sentences as a slim silver thread, something like spider web, but strong as steel. I imagined those silver threads stitching Noah back together, stitching us back together. Each one of those *Noah Filkins is an amazing lover*s felt like a small act of kindness, an intimacy.

Then one day, after months of daily pages of *Noah Filkins is an amazing lover*s, I stopped writing them. Just stopped. Enough was enough. I felt done. Maybe I just wanted to see if Noah would say something. Maybe I just wanted to hear that Noah missed the sentences and wanted more.

I didn't hear that, not for a very long time.

*

On his deathbed, Noah looked like a raw prawn. His back had curved. He was hairless and pale and thin. Everywhere I looked, I saw thin blue veins running through his flesh. As Noah lay dying, I could look right inside him. The visible Noah. I watched his blood moving through him as he died. It was the cancer that did it. You know the story. You've heard it before. He was ninety-two.

I got to be with him as he went. In Noah's hospital room, medical equipment hummed and beeped, and nurses came in and out, in and out, every few minutes a nurse. But none of that mattered. What mattered was the cool of Noah's hand in mine as I sat next to his hospital bed. What mattered were the questions Noah asked me: "You're ready to sell the house, right? You've talked to my insurance agent, right? You know you don't have to be alone, right? You know I don't expect that, don't want that."

I patted Noah's hand as he spoke. I said, "Yes. Yes. Yes."

Then Noah took a deep breath, turned his face toward the ceiling and said, "You almost finished with those billion sentences?"

Noah Filkins is an amazing lover. The words bloomed in my head like the melody of a nearly forgotten song. "Almost," I lied to my dying husband.

"Well, make sure you finish."

"I will," I promised my dying husband.

Then Noah closed his eyes and told me he was going to take a little nap. But we both knew it was not a nap. I watched him, for ten minutes, maybe fifteen, watched the blood in his veins still.

Before I left him, I stood and kissed him on the forehead then whispered in his ear, over and over again, "Noah Filkins, I love you." And as I whispered, I moved my index finger across his thigh, tracing into his flesh a down payment on the words I owed him: *NOAH FILKINS IS AN AMAZING LOVER.*

*

Don't let their fun shoes and professional smiles fool you. The nurses can be a hard bunch.

When I first moved into the center things were pretty good. I missed cooking for myself, and, of course, I missed Noah, every day I missed Noah, but I had a purpose. I had my promise. I had Noah's sentences to write, or, really, our sentences. Those sentences were for both of us now, the last of our communal property.

When I first arrived at the center, I had whole days to write. After breakfast I'd come back to my room, put the shopping channel on the TV, climb into my bed with a college-ruled spiral notebook and a fine point pen and write and write. *Noah Filkins is an amazing lover. Noah Filkins is an amazing lover*, piling them up one on top of another, neat as cordwood, thirty-four to a page.

In the background pretty women on the shopping channel would talk about jewelry and vacuums, frying pans and computers and boxes of Omaha steaks they would send right to your door. Imagine that, meat through the mail. And I would only half-hear about the steaks and the rest of it because I'd hear the sentence in my head as I wrote. Sometimes my voice spoke the sentence. Sometimes Noah's voice spoke the sentence. Sometimes we spoke the sentence together, sentences became chant, sentences became an intimacy.

Most days I could fill one whole notebook. Thirty-four *Noah Filkins is an amazing lover*s X seventy pages = 2,380 sentences. Sounds like a lot until you think of dividing one billion by 2,380. I never did have the heart to do the math. *Don't think about it,* I told myself. *Just listen, listen to the next sentences and the next and the next.*

One sentence at a time I filled notebook after notebook. I always kept a stack of ten or so blank ones on the nightstand on the left side of my bed. I piled the filled ones on the floor on the right side of the bed. And every night that pile was just a little higher or a little wider than it had been the night before, a jumble of *Noah Filkins is an amazing lover*s creeping like kudzu throughout my little room.

There's satisfaction in that kind of work, joy in tangible progress. You don't get that in teaching, not often. You don't get that that often in love, not really.

But then some of the nurses started asking questions. I think at first they were just trying to be friendly. Friendly is part of their job. "Whatcha doing there, Mrs. Filkins?" they'd say.

"Just writing," I'd say.

"Whatcha writing?"

"Words. Sentences," I'd say. Two questions must have been their quota for friendliness because after that they'd leave me alone, wander off somewhere. Probably to ask some other resident two questions. Questions distributed like aspirin. Two for you and two for you and two for you.

But then one day a doctor appeared, a squat balding man with a belly like a beer keg, and he had questions. Questions about wouldn't I be happier if I got out more. Questions about wouldn't it be nice to clear out some of the notebooks and have a bit more space in my room. Questions about how I felt about Noah.

It was the nurses who called the doctor. I'm sure of it. I'm sure curiosity got the best of one of them once when I was out of my room eating, and I'm sure that nurse snooped through my notebooks. And I'm sure that nurse told other nurses, and I'm sure they all decided they needed to alert the doctor. And I'm sure they huddled and whispered about me, probably smiling the whole time. I'm sure they whispered words like *hoarding* and *compulsion*, like *crazy* and *OCD*. Sometimes I wonder if they ever whispered *heartbroken*. I know they never whispered *promise*.

So when the doctor spoke with me, I just agreed. "Yes, I really should get out more. Yes, less clutter would be lovely." And when he asked about Noah, I just ignored him and kept on agreeing. "I hear some of the women have a book club. I think I'd really enjoy a book club. I'd like to start clearing out some of the notebooks today if that's possible. Is there a way to make sure they are recycled?" And I smiled the whole time. Not a professional smile, but good enough. It worked. That afternoon two nurses came with a big blue trash can to help me clean up my sentences, and I started spending time in the dayroom. It seemed like *Wheel of Fortune* was always on the TV.

*

Inside my dresser drawers, under my t-shirts, under my bras and panties.

On the backside of Jinny's paintings that hang in the lobby.

On the bottom of every table in the cafeteria.

Under the TV in the dayroom.

Inside the battery compartment of the TV's remote control.

In the pages of the phonebook nobody uses anymore.

In the Bible in the dayroom, woven among Old Testament verses no one reads anymore.

Inside the hot air vents.

Inside the cold air returns.

One the back of every plate over every outlet and every switch.

On the bottom of my bedframe.

On the underside of my sink.

This place is infested, crawling with *Noah Filkins is an amazing lovers*, each one written in black Sharpie, each one built of wavering letters formed by an ancient hand plagued by the imperative to work quickly, to get the letters all out before anyone sees. Look behind the fire extinguishers hanging in the halls. You'll find herds of them. Pick up any of the potted plants; look on the bottom of the pot. You'll find some. There may even be more, on the undersides of leaves, maybe, buried in the damp soil, maybe.

Noah Filkins is an amazing lover is a part of this place now. Like the insulation in the walls and the water flowing through the pipes, *Noah Filkins is an amazing lover* surrounds me, sustains me.

It's slow work now. Stealth costs quantity. But that's okay. I've got time. Slow and steady. I'll keep going until I'm done. Call the Sharpie factory. Call the birthday cake bakers. Let em' all know, we all got years of work ahead of us.

They'll be here soon, the local news people, the painted and polished TV ladies, the rumpled newspapermen. Just like they came last year for 106, just like they've come every year since 101. They'll come as I'm finishing my cake, and they will all ask the same question they asked last year and the year before that and the year before that: "What's the secret to a long life?"

They'll want me to smile into their cameras and say something charming and just a bit risqué. They'll want me to say, "The secret to a long life is an apple every day and two shots of whiskey every night," or something like that. But I won't.

When they ask, I'll tell them the truth, again. The secret to a long life is a promise to be kept that you carry in the center of your chest. The secret to a long life is a lover that only you can make whole.

And There Came Forth a Great Fish

LARGEST FRESHWATER
FISH.
This European catfish mea-
sured up to 11 feet long and
weighed about 565 pounds.
--Guinness Book of
World Records, 1978

One leg over the bridge guardrail. A moment of straddling. The girl imagines herself riding a horse into a fire. The second leg over the guardrail. And one big step. That really is all it takes.

Wind whistles in the girl's ears as the bridge recedes above her, its metal girders cutting the sky into triangle segments. Sky becomes a mosaic. She pins her arms to her sides hoping to speed her descent. Girl becomes a bomb.

Her sneakers puncture the still surface of the lake, a sound like shattering glass, and as the water takes her in, her ripples skate above her, out past the bridge, out to the horizon.

*

It's an old story. The big first step. The willful move into the tumultuous unknown. The hero's journey. It's an old story. It's not this story.

*

The girl feels the water entering her. It soaks her skin, assaults her eyes. It snakes into her ears, fills her nostrils. It tickles her under her

113

chin, coaxing her to open her mouth. Like a kitten scratching at the door, the water wants in.

The girl sees the fish, huge and listless as a blimp, wide-set eyes big and dull as dinner plates. The fish swims toward the girl. Its barbels wave like accusing, skeletal fingers.

Inches from the girl the great fish transforms, nature's magic. Ta-dah. Eyes gone. Barbels gone. The great fish becomes a gaping mouth, becomes a blackhole lined with rows of razor-wire teeth.

The girl tumbles headfirst, helpless, hopeful, into the darkness.

*

It's an old story. The big first step. The willful move into the tumultuous unknown, a tumble into the primal. Man's return to nature. It's an old story. It's not this story.

*

The girl can't even tell up from down, darkness thick as a wool blanket. For a moment she imagines she has returned to the womb. Girl becomes fetus. Fish becomes mother.

The girl gropes the air, hopes her fingertips might reveal the world around her. Something slick and wet and bumpy, its gives slightly when she pushes against it, makes a noise like the squish of a damp sponge. The girl brings her hands back to her face. They smell like stale whiskey. They smell like raw meat. When she licks them they taste like iron.

*

It's an old story. The big first step. The willful move into the tumultuous unknown, a tumble into the primal. Complete consumption. Exploration. The stranger in a strange land. It's an old story. It's not this story.

*

A sudden zig, a sharp zag. Movement, a rushing through space, a sound like water whooshing toward a drain surrounds the girl. The great fish spirals through the water. The great fish spirals through the water circulating on a rotating planet. The great fish spirals through the water circulating on a rotating planet spinning laps around the closest star, so many circles, and the girl is along for the ride. Helpless, hopeful, the girl just wants to hold on, just wants to feel it all spin.

*

It's an old story. The big first step. The willful move into the tumultuous unknown, a tumble into the primal. Complete consumption. Exploration. Recognition. The hero wrestles fear. The hero confronts themself. It's an old story. It's not this story.

*

The girl knows the fish now, knows the fish the way she knows her own breath. She knows where the fish is going. She knows what happens next.

They will travel to the deepest part of the lake, girl and fish, dive down, down, down, dive beyond the reach of sunbeams, dive until they settle on the soft clay bottom, darkness all around them thick and comforting as a wool blanket.

The clay of the bottom will smell like compost, like decay reborn, death become life. In the soft clay bottom they will dig, flap fins, churn tail, until they settle into the clay, until they have dug out a place of their own, until they wear the planet on their back.

And then they will shake, together, and they will feel it, a wobble in the eternal spinning circles. They will feel the whole world spinning a bit differently while they shake together.

*

It's an old story. The big first step. The willful move into the tumultuous unknown, a tumble into the primal, consumption, exploration, recognition, communion. It's an old story. It's a love story. It's this story. This is a love story.

Acknowledgements

Thanks to all the lit journal folks who gave homes to these stories in their earlier forms, especially Katey Schultz, John Carr Walker, Susan Lerner, Cathy Ulrich, and the whole *Phantom Drift* team, who all went above and beyond to support and promote my work.

Thanks to everyone at Gateway Literary Press, especially Joe Baumann. Your optimism, efficiency, and kindness made this book a book.

Thanks to the Arrowmont School of Arts and Crafts 2016 Pentaculum crew. Your enthusiasm during our week together was the secret sauce that first made this project feel like a book.

Thanks to the Arrowmont School of Arts and Crafts 2019 Pentaculum crew. Your feedback and questions were invaluable as I worked through revisions.

Thanks to Mom for all trips to the Saint Joseph County Public Library and to Dad for the joy he found in funny, folkish stories.

Thanks to the late-70s Scholastic Book Club. What would I have to write about if I hadn't been able to order the *Guinness Book of World Records* and have it shipped to my third-grade classroom?

Thanks to Mayah, Mayah's Ghost, and Beans, the dogs under my desk as I wrote these stories.

And thanks always to Kyoko. If there's any magic in these stories, it's because I have the privilege of living everyday surrounded by magic, the magic of your quick laugh, the magic of your boundless heart.

Stories in this collection previously appeared in the following magazines:

"Dead Weight" in *(b)OINK*

"Apple Stories," "Ponko Returns," and "Squeal" in *Phantom Drift*

"Mouse Drawer" in *Pilgrimage*

"Hercules Massis" in *Bite: An Anthology of Flash Fiction*

"Faith and Fight" in *Litro*

"Incandescence" in *The Molotov Cocktail*

"Lightning Woman Takes Three Lovers" in a slightly different form under the title "Lightning Woman" in *Bop Dead City*

"Holding Sampson" in *Black Dandy*

"Hot-Dog Queen" in *Little Patuxent Review*

"Loving Providers" in *Far Off Places*

"The Mulberry Tree" in *The Fourth River*

"R.J. Becomes a Piston" in *Jellyfish Review*

"Mrs. Cinnamon" in *Paper Darts*

"Sousathon" in *Barrelhouse*

"Judy's Pitch" in *Bartleby Snopes*

"Noah Filkins Is an Amazing Lover" in *Booth*

"And There Came Forth a Great Fish" in *Pidgeonholes*

Tom Weller has been a factory worker, a Peace Corps volunteer in Chad, a Planned Parenthood sexuality educator, a college writing teacher, an adult education tutor, and a workforce development workshop instructor. His short stories, flash fiction, and essays have appeared in a wide variety of literary journals including *Booth*, *Barrelhouse*, *Pidgeonholes*, *Epiphany*, *Milk Candy Review*, and *Phantom Drift*. He is a native Hoosier currently living in Victoria, Texas, and can be found on Twitter @WellerTom1.

Robin Basalaev-Binder is a visual and tattoo artist based in Montreal, Canada. They explore themes of urban and nature through watercolors, ink, and digital media. More of Robin's work can be found on their Instagram @vueloarts and @robinbbtattoo.

CPSIA information can be obtained
at www.ICGtesting.com
Printed in the USA
LVHW022157060222
710389LV00021B/3588